LAKE SONG

GRACE PALEY PRIZE FOR SHORT FICTION

LAKE SONG

A Novel in Stories

Lesley Pratt Bannatyne

MAD CREEK BOOKS, AN IMPRINT OF
THE OHIO STATE UNIVERSITY PRESS
COLUMBUS

This book is the winner of the 2024 Grace Paley Prize for Short Fiction, part of the Association of Writers & Writing Programs (AWP) Award Series. AWP is a nonprofit organization dedicated to amplifying the voices of writers and the academic programs and organizations that serve them. Please visit www.awpwriter.org for more information.

Library of Congress Cataloging-in-Publication Data
Names: Bannatyne, Lesley Pratt author
Title: Lake song : a novel in stories / Lesley Pratt Bannatyne.
Description: Columbus : Mad Creek Books, an imprint of The Ohio State University Press, 2025. | Series: Grace Paley prize for short fiction |Summary: "A collection of linked stories set in the fictional town of Kinder Falls in the Finger Lakes region of New York state. Spanning decades and generations, the stories plumb the complexities, violence, and compassion of small-town life as well as the power of the places that shape us"— Provided by publisher.
Identifiers: LCCN 2025013333 | ISBN 9780814259542 paperback | ISBN 9780814284261 ebook
Subjects: BISAC: FICTION / Literary | FICTION / Short Stories (single author) | LCGFT: Short stories | Novels
Classification: LCC PS3602.A666 L35 2025 | DDC 813/.6—dc23/eng/20250414
LC record available at https://lccn.loc.gov/2025013333

Cover design by Nathan Putens
Text design by Juliet Williams
Type set in Adobe Sabon LT Pro

For Sans Souci and all it holds

Contents

4. LAKE SONG

1

BURNED OVER

Desire covered the land like winter—demanding, unyielding, beatific—like the miles of low hills that stretched westward, uninterrupted by mill or derrick or brick. It was this torn pocket of west central New York that the angel Moroni led Joseph Smith Jr. to Hill Cumorah to receive the golden plates that would become the Book of Mormon. Here, visions came to Mother Ann Lee's Shakers, to Jemima Wilkinson and her Universal Friends, and to teenager Maggie Fox and her little sister Kate, who unwittingly birthed Spiritualism in their bedroom. It was called the burned-over district because there wasn't a single soul who hadn't been set on fire by religion.

The resources of the natural world lay beneath their feet and the kingdom of heaven above their heads, and it was this bounty that encouraged the people who lived here to move in any direction, or any dimension, that brought them closer to the divine. It made them more susceptible, perhaps, to the grifters and wayward who followed the saints; but also to the inexplicable, the miraculous, and the glorious.

It is here that you find a sprawl of lakes dug deep in the rock. Okisee was the smallest of these, and the town of Kinder Falls sprang up around it: first squatter's shacks, then houses, barns, stores, autos, sidewalks, electricity. The town grew, languished, prospered, suffered, boomed, settled. Throughout it all, people watched the reflection of evening in the water:

orange-pink-gray-dark-stars. They listened to the loon's wail, fish thrashing for insects, waves ticking off the minutes, hours, before bed. The lake gave all these. But the lake also took: wedding rings, china, boats, watches, keys, glasses, shoes, bones, oars, tarps, umbrellas, towels, toys, shovels, wagon wheels, horseshoes, rope, spoons, pipes, canes, and souls—drunken, confused, or misled.

The lake was a diary. Wind turned the pages; canoes floated like commas.

Coaxing Sugar from the Trees

1906

Mavis

Mavis's daddy had been dead only three months when all three Epps brothers came by her house to ask what she was going to do with the twenty-two acres of woods her father had sugared since she was born, and she told them it was none of their business. They said they'd offer her more money than she could earn sugaring, and she said over my dead body, and on the way out the youngest brother, Angus Epps, called back, it's a real shame, Mavis Staunch, you were such a pretty girl when you were young. She was twenty-six.

Mavis didn't care for any of the Epps brothers. Their hands were thick-fingered, and they had a way of moving—eel-like, as if their bones were soft—that made them look lazy even when they were working. She shoved her canoe into Okisee Lake and dipped her paddle deep, pulled hard, which felt good, the sensation of muscle working wood through water. The lake lay black beneath her, but the moon shed a pale smear across its surface. She peered over the side. There in the deep was her twin, ageless, hair loose and frizzed in the night's dampness, dark circle of a mouth. Above her, busyness in the stars: the bears, mother and child, inching south in the spring sky, soon to be trailed by hunters; the water snake, long and ghostly.

Mavis ticked off what needed tending to in the morning.

The maple water was rising—March already—so she'd check her trees. Next, she would speak to the Tuttle boy's parents. An awful boy, their Harley, square-headed and fat with hair like bleached knotgrass. He'd been fishing this morning and Mavis slid across his line in her canoe. She hadn't noticed it, or him, and he'd yelled at her to get away. A child scolding a grown woman!

A maddened yowling erupted in the distance—coyotes after a raccoon or opossum. Then an awful snarling and the screams of an animal in pain. She tried to ignore the cries of the poor, unlucky creature.

Early the next morning Mavis walked the quarter mile to Tuttle's home and called hello from the backyard. The house was silent. Someone drew the kitchen curtains closed. Mavis lifted the pitchfork that rested against the porch and slammed it against the side of the house until an enormously pregnant girl appeared at the door. You need to know, Annalee, she said, that your brother addressed me in the rudest way yesterday. A child does not speak to an adult like that. He needs to be punished. The girl's mouth opened and closed, like a guppy.

Satisfied she'd been heard, Mavis climbed the dirt road that snaked uphill from the lake where the houses grew smaller and hard worn. A large stone at the side of the road marked a deer path that meandered through the north edge of her property. Mavis was happy to see small depressions in the snow dotting the base of each maple; the roots were warming. Her father's voice whispered in her ear: *tap on the south side for the sun. Don't tap the young trees, don't tap the very old. They'll let you know.*

A week after their visit to her, the Epps brothers summoned

Mavis to the office of John Beck, the town of Kinder Falls' only attorney. In 1906 the town was growing—Bull's Tavern, Brouwer's General Store, the Presbyterian church, the Congregational church, post office, bank, Singer's, a cafeteria, and a block of offices shielded by dirty glass windows. Beck's was the largest. The two married Epps brothers sat in high-backed chairs like bishops in soiled, button-front shirts. Angus Epps leaned against a wall with a hip slung out and both hands in his pockets. Beck stood when Mavis entered.

The Epps brothers would like to make a formal offer on your property, he said. They are looking to expand their hops fields and—you'll like this, Mavis—they'll pay you a higher price than what they offered before. Maybe you'll reconsider? Beck cocked his head and raised his eyebrows.

Mavis's eyes darted around the office. Beck's fur-collared overcoat hung on a nail. The curling print of a Yates County map showed the grid of roads designed as the "military plan." On Beck's desk there were papers, a few nails, a pipe, an inkwell. It was a man's place and it smelled of men: leather shoes, sweat, tobacco, dust.

I'm not interested in selling my land.

Beck leaned in toward Mavis. At some point, Mavis, he said kindly, your land may be more trouble than it's worth.

I can take care of it, Beck.

Angus Epps stared at her, his hands playing with his belt buckle, tomcat-like. He was a mess of a man, wet around the lips.

Things are changing, Beck said, quietly. Sugar's cheaper from the Indies now and people don't need your syrup like before. You're going to start losing money on your trees; cost you more firewood to keep the boil going than gallons you can sell. It's a good offer, Mavis.

Thank you, Beck, Mavis said, but no. I own the last piece

of uncut forest around Kinder Falls, and I'd like to keep it
that way. She rose and nodded at the married brothers, now
slumped in their chairs like old dogs. She didn't look at Angus.
Your offer is generous and I appreciate that, but no. Good day,
gentlemen.

Okisee Lake was a half-mile wide and nearly two miles long,
edged with a beach of water-smoothed shale. Each morning before dawn, Mavis ran naked across the stones into the
water and swam, arm over arm, until she couldn't stand the
cold another second, then sprinted, red-thighed and breathless, back to the house where the woodstove was already lit,
and she could sit naked until her body warmed. Every morning
from the start of sugaring she did this. Her grandmother had
done it, and her mother too.

This morning, as Mavis sat by the stove drying her hair,
she heard whistling out on the road that ran by her house. She
lifted her kitchen curtain and spied Harley Tuttle carrying a
puppy, a squirming, yelping, black-and-white mutt. The boy
lost hold of it and the puppy bolted, tail wagging so hard it
could barely run. It rooted through the chicory, through the
stout, sharp stubble that covered the roadside, dug down into
a clump of stalks, winced, pulled away, tried a different angle.
Mavis smiled to herself. That's what a pup is, that's what it
does.

Lincoln! the boy called. Lincoln, come! He ran after the
dog, snatched him up.

Lincoln, Mavis thought. She liked the name. Mavis stuffed
her pipe and closed her kitchen curtain tight. Didn't want anyone seeing her smoking.

Come afternoon, she walked the half mile to Brouwer's grocery to buy lard, where Mrs. Brouwer told her that the old jus-

tice of the peace had died in the night and would be waked in three days, and it wasn't going to be easy to bury him with the ground half-frozen. No, Mavis agreed. The bell on the front door jangled and Angus Epps slid in. Mavis took her purchase, gave Angus a curt nod, and hurried out of the store.

The day was graying and a chilly wind came up from the south and pushed against her. Halfway home, she heard footfalls following behind. Angus. She quickened her pace. Angus quickened his. A hot flush rose up the back of Mavis's neck despite the breeze. Leaves blew silver, their undersides flipping up. When she reached her yard Mavis turned to face him.

Angus Epps, she said, forcing a smile. What do you want?

Eyes like wet rocks. He took a wobbly step closer and gave Mavis a hungry look. Drunk. I seen you in the water, he said.

Mavis's smile vanished. She put her head down, entered her kitchen, shut the door tight, and latched it. Her heart drummed against her ribs. She watched Angus through the window, an unsteady figure in her yard.

I seen you, Angus called.

Get along, Angus, Mavis said, louder.

To her shock, Angus walked onto her porch and threw all his weight against the door. The latch flew off. His eyes raked her breasts, her belly.

The hawk circled on a southerly wind, eyes locked on motion in the weeds. He made a tighter circle above the treetops, taking in scents of wood smoke and kerosene, ears tuned to the chipmunk racing toward a pile of stones. The hawk chose its moment, dove, speared the chipmunk's back body with its talons and circled up, aware but uninterested in the frantic banging of Mavis's fist against her bedroom wall.

Mavis twisted her head away from Angus and bucked

against his weight, against his hands pinning hers, slippery
with sweat, his fingers squeezing rhythmically. Mavis shut her
eyes tight but she could still see his hands. Dirty fingernails,
yellow knuckles. And she could smell him. She tried to hold
her breath but his weight on her chest made her gasp. She bit
at his face like a snapping dog, missing. She grunted, hissed,
spit. She refused to cry out.

At last he lifted off her, drew up his trousers and stood at
the end of the bed. Mavis stayed motionless until she heard
the door shut behind him and his footsteps fade. She took a
careful breath; to fill her lungs again felt like it might split her
ribs. She touched her feet to the floor and stood up, holding
onto the cedar chest for balance. Her bloomers fell around
her ankles. She kicked them off. She smoothed down her dress
and walked out of the house and across the stony beach into
the lake, feeling frigid water on her calves, the slippery green
rocks beneath her feet. Waist deep, her skirt floated around
her; chest deep, it sank and dragged as she fought its weight
to take another step, and another. She lay back and kicked her
legs wide to get rid of him. The dress spread out around her,
black against black water. She let herself sink down below the
surface and looked skyward. The dry world was still there, but
dimly. Mavis planted her feet on the lake's bottom and walked
back to shore. Her dress clung to her skin, tangled up in her
legs, and took on the chill of evening. A seagull perched on a
rock and stared at Mavis, beak hanging open like a drunken
farmer.

She dumped her clothes in the wash bucket, pulled her
nightgown over her head, and sat by the wood stove to think,
but she couldn't settle. She got up and tore her quilt from the
bed and threw it into the tub as well. Sat back down. Rocked.
Poked at the fire. Opened the silverware drawer and pulled
out all but one of her knives. She placed a knife by the back

door, one by the front door, one out in the privy. She found her father's tackle box and took the fish knife—small enough that it could be hidden under a waistband or in the palm of a hand—and put it next to her bed.

Though Mavis Staunch's house was a hundred yards from the Brouwer's on one side, and across a creek and just as far from the Tuttle's on the other, these homes were lakeside and water carried sound. On snow-quiet evenings, Mavis could hear Cal Tuttle load split logs into his stove. In the summer when doors and windows were open, she could hear old Margaret Brouwer pissing in her chamber pot. Sound carried the most clearly in the dampness of evening. Because of that, because it was late spring and coming on dusk, Mavis knew everyone had heard. She wanted to burn off her own hide. To take a mouthful of lye and let it eat away all the parts that had been dirtied.

Mavis stood at the kitchen window listening to the sounds of what only this morning had been comfort: shuffle in the leaves, lap of waves, resettling of stones at the water's edge. But then, out of the quiet erupted a frantic yipping of coyotes, close and coming closer. She saw thrashing in the bushes, then three of them—frenzied, snarling—broke through the brush chasing some poor, limping thing. They tumbled into her yard, jumping over each other to sink teeth and tear. Mavis grabbed the shovel she kept outside her back door. Go! she screamed, charging at the coyotes, shovel raised high. Get! Go! She slammed the shovel down on the ground. The coyotes circled, whining, reluctant to leave their prize. She thrust the shovel toward them, swung it, and hit one on the rump. They jittered and ran toward the road, all three.

The creature lay at her feet, bloodied and limp. Oh, no, Mavis breathed. No. The puppy was split open and its insides heaved out onto the ground, its breath coming fast and shallow. Lincoln looked up at her with pleading eyes. Mavis raised her shovel above her head and slammed it down, once, twice.

She covered Lincoln's body with a canvas tarp to keep animals away. Shaking, Mavis got into her canoe and shoved off. She'd go to the Tuttle's tomorrow and tell them what had happened. They would bury Lincoln properly. She tried to fill her lungs but she couldn't get enough air in. She was dizzy and the night chilled her. She thought of overturning the canoe and feeling the icy water on every inch of her skin, inside her mouth, her ears. She thought of diving down and swimming as far as her arms would take her. God was angry and cruel and was responsible for coyotes and Angus Epps. And God was water and starlight and the trees hewn into curved ribs that floated her in the middle of the lake. All of it. Good and bad didn't come close to describing Him.

The Tuttle boy and his father came the next afternoon. The father nodded to Mavis and gathered up the bundle in a towel he'd brought from home. The boy stared at her with so much hate Mavis had to concentrate to keep her hands still. He could only be ten or so; too young to be so angry.

As soon as they left, Mavis hurried to the sugar shack where her hired workers, an Irish family called McCallum, had begun tapping the trees. She made a show of counting the empty jugs, thirty-two, but she was really looking for the youngest McCallum, Tom. She needed to see the little boy, to feel his slightness in her lap. Tom, with eyes that reflected the sky, so blue, and auburn hair that turned deep red at sunset. Tom, who was all good and nothing else.

Mrs. McCallum emerged from the shack.

Tom around? Mavis asked.

Mrs. McCallum took one look at Mavis and wrapped an

arm around her shoulders and held her until the snakes under Mavis's skin stilled. Tom! she called. Miss Mavis has come to see you.

The boy jumped from a tree and ran to Mavis, who plopped down on the ground so he could climb on her. She pulled on his fat earlobes and he giggled, a sound so beautiful her heart swelled. Had she been a mother once? She felt at that moment that there could be a woman flitting around inside the woman Mavis was, putting flowers in jars, cleaning windows, baking little cakes. For the first time since Angus, she took in a full breath. Maybe they needed another teacher at the grade school. She was young yet, and unmarried, a plus.

For the rest of the day Harley watched Mavis like a spy, plotting. He watched her through her kitchen window, sitting next to the stove drying her hair. Dog murderer. Witch. How the boy hated her. Her sickly white forehead with its dark eyebrows like a man's and her skin so slimy it looked like butcher paper and her ugly hair that grew in all directions and wasn't any color he could name: rust, tin, mud? He daydreamed about taking his father's rifle and shooting Mavis dead, shooting her right in her own kitchen but that seemed too kind because she wouldn't suffer, so he thought about standing over Mavis with a shovel raised above his head, listening to her beg him to spare her and imagining her body stiff as a squirrel run over by a milk truck.

That night Harley woke to moonlight shining through his bedroom window. The house was quiet, other than the familiar sounds: his mother's soft snoring, the rooster-like call of a hoot owl. He rose out of bed. Something drew him to the lakefront—a splashing in the water. He bent into the shadows cast by the twin pines in front of his house and he saw her:

Mavis Staunch in her canoe, paddling toward the lake's center. It struck him instantly, like God himself had whispered in his ear. He knew exactly what to do.

Mavis dressed carefully for the justice's wake. She was not going to let what happened keep her from paying her respects; she'd been fond of him. When she was a girl, he drove Mavis and her grandmother to Spiritualist tent meetings in Bethel. Mavis loved these meetings; she loved to watch the men and women who came forward to hear words from their dead wives, mothers, and most often, their children. *I'm happy here. There are lots of boys and girls to play with. It didn't hurt.* She found comfort among these strangers who hoped, as she did, that there was an unseen world wrapped around this one where all the souls who had ever lived waited, open-armed and joyful. Hello Mama. Hello Papa. She hoped the justice was at peace there, with his people.

She pushed a dozen tiny buttons at her waist through their buttonholes. From neck to bosom, another blizzard of buttons. Underneath, two petticoats, knotted tight. Mavis used to dress for comfort; now she dressed for protection. Every hook hooked, every button secured, shoes laced and double-knotted. She drew her pearl choker around her neck, pinched the clasp, and walked the four miles to the justice's house, carrying the mulberry pie she'd made. Spring was such a sad time to die, Mavis thought, with everything waking up and moving in the world. Afternoon sun set its rays down on the lake like ribbons.

The old man had left the world neatly, like a freshly ironed sheet put away in a dresser. He lay in a pine casket, hands clasped calmly on his chest, his boiled Dutch skin translucent. The justice's wife moved food around on a small table in the second room. She looked worn bare with grief. Mavis touched the woman's shoulder. The justice's wife smiled. Then she realized who Mavis was and her face went flat. She moved away to the stove. The light in the room darkened as a cloud passed the sun and the crowd of a dozen faded to silhouette. Mavis knew them all: Bethany Chaddam from the Yates County Bank, Herk Ernst who raised sheep on the west side of the lake, the elder Markys, married so long they hung on each other like old sweaters. She tried to find one person she could talk with so she wasn't standing alone in the room, but she couldn't make a soul meet her eyes, even the boy they called Jep, whose pants were too short and who couldn't keep his feet still, even while he was eating. The way they didn't look at her made her feel huge, as if she took up too much space. Mavis sensed the women were wary of her, as if her new carnality made her dangerous around their men and daughters. And the men—Mavis knew they would be thinking about her body, what she'd done, had been done to her.

She said a quick "Our Father" over the justice's body and left the house. Clouds in the north filled up darkly and within minutes shot out a rain so sharp it stung. She stood under the awning of the apothecary shop for respite. Across the street, Angus Epps argued with his brother, then stormed off toward the edge of town. Mavis waited a bit, then put her head down and let the rain drench her, hurt her, as she walked, her fist curled around the handle of her father's fish knife, just in case.

Harley Tuttle waited until he saw Mavis leave for the justice's wake. He snuck behind her house to the canoe, stored bottom-up against the coming rain. He worked his jackknife hard into the side until it came through the canvas shell. Then he worked the cut, starting at what would be the water line and sawing down a few inches. A long, almost invisible cut. Took him some time. Clouds thickened and darkened. A drop came, then more, then a steady rain. He did the same on the other side of the boat, higher up, toward the stern. And two more on each side. Six cuts. The boat would leak slowly through the first cuts, but as it took on water and grew heavier, the lake would find the rest. The cutting felt noble.

Mavis was exhausted. She dried off and lay down fully dressed but couldn't sleep. Each time she drifted off—there was a green bird flapping its wings against her window, her papa tapping ashes from a pipe, a tiny curl twitching in the hair of little Tom—she jerked herself awake, as if she didn't deserve the dream. After many hours she gave up, buttoned up her coat and went to the lake. The rain had stopped, and a hem of foam hugged the shore. She shoved her canoe into the water and stroked hard until she was in the center. The boat rocked lightly. She peered into the deep dark below, searching for her twin, the pretty one, the sweet one. No moon, no reflection, only a blackness that reached to the bottom where the fish were blind from lack of light.

The hem of her skirt was damp. Her boots too. Dew, she thought. She leaned back, rested her feet on the gunwales and closed her eyes. The lapping of water against the canoe lulled her and she drifted, dreaming of dresses in colors she'd never seen before; a blue the color of sapphire, of sea holly blooms; bright pink; luminous orange. A robin flitted somewhere up in the rafters. A choir sang in a place far away from her. But then, a loon's wild laugh. Mavis sat up. How long had she been asleep?

There were five inches of water in the boat. Panicking, she knelt and ran her hand over the ribs to feel where the water was coming in; she found a long, thin cut. She held her fingers against the breach but could feel water seeping from another leak on the opposite side. She held both hands against the holes, but the boat was now filling faster.

Hallo! She called out. Help! Please! Hallo!! The lake was deserted. It was a quarter mile to shore. Mavis knew she could swim it unless the cold slowed her. She wriggled out of her coat—too heavy—and tried to pull off her boots but couldn't; her laces were knotted and wet. She tried to take off her dress, but the buttons were tiny and her hands too cold to work them. She couldn't tear it apart; the garment was well made and the cotton tightly woven. Her beloved canoe was only inches above water. Mavis rolled out of it and took a few strong strokes toward shore. Arm over arm, breathing hard, she swam. Her skirt, monster that it was, wrapped itself around her legs as she tried to kick. She stroked harder with her arms and dragged her lower body along. Arm over arm over arm over arm. Her legs grew heavy, her movements sluggish. Mavis no longer felt the cold, and at that, she was surprised.

Margaret Brouwer heard the shouts and roused her husband, who ran from his house, hollering for his sons to come. Margaret stood on the shore in her nightdress, pointing, frantic for them to move faster.

It's Mavis out there, hurry!

The three men, father and two grown sons, shoved off in a dinghy and rowed hard toward the middle of the lake. From the Tuttle house, the father came running with a lantern, slid his rowboat into the water and oared in the direction of the sound of the Brouwer boat.

Ho, Tuttle!

Ho!

We heard her before, one of the Brouwer sons called. Somewhere around here.

In the dark center of Okisee, the two boats rocked. Tuttle raised his lantern high. Can't see a damn thing, he said.

No stars, Brouwer answered.

No wind, even.

Awful still.

The men listened to the lake, sensitive to any disturbance in the surface, a bubble, but the water was quiet. They waited silently until Tuttle's lantern burned out. Then they rowed back to shore.

Mavis's body stretched tall and wide. Between her fingers, little nubs of green emerged. They budded between her toes, out of her spine, and snaked from the crease in her hips. Brilliant, lush stems unfurled from every joint and reached their greenness toward the light above. She was lovely and long, and she swayed with the currents of the lake, growing ever longer and more lovely. When she reached bottom she saw that the lake floor was full of people, of beautiful quilts anchored with stones, woven baskets, blue cloth napkins. There was the old butcher with a mustache of sweat on his upper lip. There was Ben Hatch dancing by himself with his suspenders dangling off his waistband. There was the boy who kissed her ear on May Day, handsome as he was then and looking just as wicked. The old justice with his soft hands, white fingernails. Papa. Grandmother handing her plums wrapped in a napkin. And candles burning everywhere. Was it Christmas? Little Lincoln's grateful eyes, oh, sweet Lincoln. She could smell cake, vanilla and honey. And everywhere, a glorious phosphorescence. She relaxed at last and breathed in the smell of water.

A Ten-Year-Old Boy

On the night Mavis Staunch drowned, Angus Epps disappeared. Brouwer would find him the next spring when the thaw came, and creeks flooded the lake with snowmelt that pushed the bones of dead cows, deer, foxes, and Angus Epps into Okisee. Most people figured he'd fallen off the train trestle bridge only a mile from his family farm. Others had questions about that.

On the night Mavis drowned, Mrs. Tuttle had to settle her boy Harley with a whiskey pour. He wouldn't look at her, at his sister, at anyone. It was queer, the way his index finger rubbed his thumb, insect-like. Mrs. Tuttle held him tight in her arms, but he was ice cold and sweating all at once. The boy was never quite right again, and Mr. Tuttle had to move his family down the waterfront another half mile to where they had some privacy.

A ten-year-old boy doesn't know that things change.
  If it's snowing, it will always be snowing.
  If it's summer, it will always be summer.
  This thing he did will be a thing that he did forever.
  For a ten-year-old boy, the night is never still and the night is never silent.

The loon laughs at him and he lets it.
Because of all this he becomes small.
He stays still in silences.
He breathes thinly, as through a straw.
He doesn't make noise with his feet.
He doesn't hold his sister's baby, ever.
He becomes a carp, a bottom feeder, waiting for leftover bits that sink to the lake floor.
He becomes the color of water.

The Stone House

1930

Harley

Before a storm the air turns opaque, barely gray, and the wind changes direction. In the distance where the gray is thicker, tiny whitecaps lick the surface of the lake. Boats are pulled up higher onto the shore, windows cranked shut, chairs tied down. Bird chatter escalates. Lilac branches lift and settle, lift and settle. The horizon disappears, the lake shortens, the world diminishes, and the storm's ferocious white comes in; it is the dirty white of opossum, the thick white of milk. Harley Tuttle hides his terror of storms, of water, in his fingers. He's grown up, despite everything.

Harley left Kinder Falls the day after he turned twenty-one and found work up north in a fish processing plant on Lake Ontario. Thick calluses formed on the slope between his thumb and index finger. Frostbite took two of his toes in the winter of snow-after-snow, which kept him from President Wilson's war; in cold weather he dragged them along, limp, dead cousins to his other toes. But his hands held his guilt perfectly, and the only time he could keep them still was when he held something useful. A rake. A fish knife. A mallet. Otherwise, his fingers rubbed against each other obsessively, giving him the appearance of a housefly cleaning itself. When the processing plant shuttered, he was happy to find work chiseling names on gravestones for Bonn's funeral home in Tug Hill, a tiny berg south of the Canadian border. No one had heard of Kinder Falls, and Okisee Lake was too small to be drawn on the map of New York State that hung in the town's barber shop. He liked that the only water in Tug Hill was a mud-clogged river that ran behind the downtown stores.

He didn't mean for Mavis to drown. He only meant to sink her canoe, like she killed his dog.

It was mercy, son, don't you see? his father had tried to explain. The animal was suffering. But Harley couldn't see. He was just a boy then. The lake was deep, and they didn't find Mavis until weeks later, when a fierce storm carried her to shore.

At night Harley still dreamt about her. Mavis, walking out of the lake, her boots clicking on the slate path that led to his room. Her eyes, shriveled like rotted stone fruit. Mavis, reaching out her arms, the ribbon sewn onto the cuffs of her dress feathered as if the lake had taken a comb to it. Mavis, stopping at his door, an eel sliding out of her mouth.

Can a man be forgiven for something a boy did?

It was early October, and the oak leaves had already crisped. A sharply thin, beak-nosed man came into Bonn's shop, hair to his shoulders like a woman's. He was dark-eyed and thick-eyebrowed, with fingernails painted blue. The man's eyes slid over the room full of carved gravestones: Righteous Mother, Loyal Servant.

Harley looked up. What can I do for you?

The man moved closer. A deep crease in his forehead. Fur hat. Harley's thumb and index finger rubbed together furiously. Harley spoke louder: Are you looking to order a stone?

The man stroked the fur collar on his coat, stared past Harley at the door to the back of the shop, and twisted a strand of hair around a long, bejeweled finger. Perhaps, he said. What's beyond that door? His voice, something metallic in it. A lilt in his sentences. Quebecois.

The owner lets it out to me. To live in. Harley grasped a stone to still one hand, picked up a rasp to calm the other.

The man palmed a chip of marble, turned it over. He peered out the window at the long dirt lane that led to the shop.

Only you?

Yes.

Bonn's monument shop was a distance from his funeral office in town so widowers, bereft mothers, brothers, and children could drive the half mile alone with their grief past a quiet line of elms to the shop's front door, which welcomed them with a bouquet of fresh flowers, replaced daily. Harley apprenticed for five years chiseling names and designs— angels, acorns, baskets, doves. He was good at it, despite the rude tools he'd been given, despite the agitation of his insect hands, despite the dust that turned his snot black. He learned patience, letter by letter. He learned how to sense weakness in brownstone, how to follow flaws in marble. He learned the size of the stone did not reflect the magnitude of grief. Baby stones were small. Father stones and banker stones were the heaviest.

The stranger looked out the back window of the shop. He smiled. And the woodshed, that is also yours to use?

Yes, Harley said.

The man wrapped one slender arm around Harley's shoulders. I'm looking for a place to store a couple dozen cases, he said. I would bring them on a Tuesday, late, and we—you and I—would hide them in the shed. My colleague will take them away the next night. Do you understand what I'm asking?

Harley moved away from him.

I'll pay you forty dollars a week.

Harley's fingers stopped moving.

The man whirled around Bonn's shop, looking out each window, running his fingers along the stones. What's this stone?

Marble.

I like it very much. It's tintless.

It's seashells.

The man raised an eyebrow. He licked a finger and picked up some stone dust, touched it to his tongue. I'll tell you this, my friend: it is a good business, liquor. Buy a bottle for $10 in Canada, walk it across the border in your pants, sell it for twenty-five dollars in America and make more in a day than you would in a week working in this shop. What I'm offering is even better, and easier too. So?

The man was the color of wet trees, standing there between Harley and the light of the window, his eyes shadowed under his hat. Harley thought about old Bonn finding out, how disappointed he'd be, how angry. Then he looked around the shop, at the tools stained dark with the sweat of his palms. At the door to his rooms, dimly lit, the pile of quilts he slept on, his awful aprons, everything covered in gray grit. He was hungry, always hungry, and cold, because the windows never shut completely and the floorboards froze his feet from September to June. His eyes fixed on the man's fur coat. What have I got to lose? he thought. He nodded. Okay.

The man let out a long hiss between his teeth and laughed. He took Harley's hand and gave it one hard shake. Remy Malveaux.

Harley Tuttle.

Well, Harley Tuttle, let me tell you this: You are a smart man. The people that hide whiskey under their floorboards, in fake gas tanks, in their lamps, books, mattresses, canes, and ladies' coats, they're not smart. There's a man in Tioga who knows how to mix whiskey with the air in the tubes of tires. Even he is not smart. This, what we will do, is smart. You'll see.

Remy half-smiled, did a quick bow, and left the shop.

Harley watched Malveaux fold himself into a yellow Hillman tourer and motor back down the rutted dirt road, made for horses, not cars.

Forty dollars.

The light in the room dimmed. Harley smelled lake water: Mavis. *Stupid man. There is always more to lose.*

Lakes disappear over time. Weeds grow thicker along the bank, seaweed fattens, water sinks down into the bed, the bed becomes a marsh, and the marsh, a field. Harley walks every inch of that field searching for Mavis's canoe. It's not there. Not a single rib or patch of canvas. He takes his chisel and hammer and digs down through the layers of mud and slate, deer bones and rock, but comes up empty. He wants to find her, beg her to forgive him. I didn't mean for it to happen. Why didn't you see that the canoe was cut? He calls for her, but his voice is lost in mud. When she does come to him, she comes without ears. She shimmers at the edge of his consciousness, a wisp of memory with no shape or weight but heavier than any stone.

The first delivery came on a Tuesday, late October but winter-cold, eleven at night. The grocer's wife wouldn't make eye contact with Harley earlier that day; did she know what he was going to do? He paid her with shaky hands. Even in his own room he had trouble lighting the stove because of his twitchy fly fingers. Every minute lagged. Even the sun stalled; it hung above the tree line forever like a kite gone dead. When darkness came at last, Harley stayed perched at his window listening to the chimes from the faraway town clock: seven, eight, nine, ten.

Finally, two pinpricks appeared in the distance. The car's headlamps bounced over ruts in the road. A tree trunk jumped out of the murk, glowed briefly, vanished. A slick sheet of frozen mud materialized as the car descended a rise. The car made a turn and went dark, headlights off for the last stretch. Harley went out to meet it. He heard the tires crunch through shallow puddles of ice, then silence, and the hulking Ford was in front of him. Black, all curves, no license plate. Malveaux emerged. To Harley's shock, the passenger door opened, and a young woman stepped outside and stretched. Remy cocked his head in her direction.

My niece, Lily.

She looked like she'd been asleep, her eyes damp, a mess of chestnut curls hanging halfway down her back. She was maybe eighteen years old and small like a gold chain was small. A thick fur coat reached to her ankles. On her feet, men's boots.

Remy nodded his head. The girl strode to the elm that sheltered the shop, and, like a young boy, leapt up to the first branch and climbed higher.

She'll watch out for us, Malveaux said. He opened the trunk of the car. That's $2,400 of Haig and Haig Scotch Whiskey, my friend. Malveaux laughed and clapped Harley on the shoulder. Shall we? Malveaux slid the first case over to Harley, who lifted it—heavy, but manageable—and brought it to the woodshed. Be graceful, Malveaux called out.

They moved the cases, breathing clouds into the frigid air. When they'd stacked the last case, Malveaux piled firewood in front of the stash and padlocked the door. The girl joined them and the three leaned against the back wall of the shop. Malveaux took a bottle from his coat and passed it around. Tomorrow night, he said, my colleague will take this away. Leave the padlock open. Don't be home.

Harley couldn't stop himself from searching the road for movement.

Malveaux chuckled. Don't be nervous, my square-headed friend, he said. There are fifty roads that lead from Montreal to the Hudson, and no one can patrol them all.

The bottle went around again. Harley stared at the starless sky. He wished the Canadian would stop talking; someone out on the road might hear them. But Malveaux wouldn't stop. He talked excitedly about using sleds on the snow, about the drivers who abandoned their cars and ran into the fields to escape the police—better to lose the load and the car than it is to lose the driver, Malveaux said—about farmers hiding liquor in haylofts. Lily barely spoke at all, and when she did it was a few words to her uncle in French.

A feral cat trotted along the shed toward them.

If you need to find gold, Malveaux said, interrupting his own monologue, you find a *chat noir* and slit its throat. The blood spurting out will tell you which direction to dig.

Harley shooed the cat away with his foot. Malveaux looked up at the full moon and howled.

Quiet! Harley hissed. His chest was tight from fear and whiskey and the girl.

Malveaux laughed, a short, nasal honk. Ten years ago whiskey was legal, he said. Now, no. But it could be legal next year, or the year after. See? It's not the whiskey that's bad. It's the law. He winked at Harley, then sauntered over to the elm to relieve himself.

Lily turned to Harley and quickly took his hands between her own. You must be cold, she said. You're shaking. Her voice was silvery, accented, something between a lullaby and a wind chime.

Harley felt the sizzle of butter in a frypan run up his spine. He jerked away and wedged his awful, twitching hands under his armpits, but his rebellious fingers continued to rub against each other. Horsefly. Mosquito. Praying mantis.

Lily slapped him lightly on the chest. You're like a little fish, she said. Cold and hard to hold.

She was beautiful in the moonlight and close enough that Harley smelled spice: clove. Could hear, he imagined, her heart tapping under her coat. He had never wanted anything more than to close his arms around her, feel the top of her head against his chin.

Lily turned her face up to the sky and hugged her coat tight around her. Look at the moon. So full.

Something brushed Harley's cheek with a frayed sleeve. He breathed in slowly though his nose to keep panic from rising up in his gullet. He smelled lake water and the salt-sulfur of rotting leaves: Mavis, again. Soundless words tunneled into his ear. *Talk to her.*

Yes, he said. The moon. Beautiful.

She likes you.

Harley didn't dare believe it. He was a stunted man, stopped up short. Cats sensed it; they wouldn't stay around, even if he fed them. He stared at his feet.

Remy reappeared and tossed his empty bottle to Harley. Anyone different come around here last week? he asked, his tone serious.

No one comes around here but the families of dead people looking for stones.

If you do notice anyone sneaking around, anybody watching you—

Harley's nerves ratcheted up. Who would be watching me?

The Klan, Lily whispered.

The Klan? Harley said. Not around here.

Remy blew a puff of air. *Non, monsieur.* They are every-where. Your minister. Your fish man. Your grocer. Your Bonn.

Harley glanced around at the road. Still empty.

Don't worry, friend. It's me they want to get rid of, not you.

They want only born-American people to be here, Lily said quietly. No Pope people.

And they hate whiskey! Remy spread his arms wide and bowed. His rings glittered and his boots shone. That's me. Canadian, Catholic, bootlegger! You want me gone? Catch me. He laughed, loud and long. Keep a sharp eye on that shed, Remy said. Anyone comes snooping around, you tell me. Even someone you know.

The next day, Harley watched the shed as he worked. Cut his palm not looking what he was doing, bled on unsealed mar-ble, cursed himself. Late that night, he left the padlock on the shed open, as instructed, and walked downtown. New wires ran off telephone poles every twenty feet, crisscrossing the street like angry stitches. Electric lights burned in a few apartments over dark shops. Above the grocery, he could see a woman silhou-etted in a window. He moved back into the shadows. The town was empty, save for a few rats and one lone dog. He walked the streets, past the cemetery, along the river, until the town clock chimed one, then he went home. The whiskey was gone.

And so it went, week after week through the winter, spring, and most of the summer. Harley's nervousness faded; he began to look forward to the deliveries. To the thrill, the camara-derie, the money. To Lily. He hadn't thought about Mavis in months. Then the heat of August set everything boiling.

August of 1931 was hotter than any other Harley could remember, and it was still early in the month. The heat was suffocating, even at night. Harley waited for Remy and Lily well past midnight, skimming the newspaper and drinking coffee. Chinese earthquake, martial law in Cuba, a no-hitter against the Red Sox. In New York City, Jack Diamond got four years in prison for bootlegging. Harley closed the paper.

It was after one when the Ford came into view. It moved slowly down the lane as if even the engine was choking in the heat. Lily was barely dressed, her sleeve slipping off a shoulder as she climbed out of the truck and took up her lookout post. She winked at Harley as she went by. She'd taken to touching him on the back, the shoulder, the cheek, whenever her uncle's attention went elsewhere. Harley lived for it. This girl, Harley believed, could wring the bad out of him. Wash him clean and hang him in the sun to cure.

Remy and Harley moved slowly, stooping, lifting, stacking, their sweat soaking through their shirts. When they'd finished, Remy sat back against the elm outside of the shop. He fanned himself with his hat and fell asleep.

Lily jumped down from her perch. Come! she whispered, and pulled on Harley's hand. They ran through a hayfield to the river that once powered the mill that had made the town famous for its falling water, but no more. They took off their shoes and stood at the edge. Every sound was amplified by the dampness of the night. The whine of a train engine struggling with too much weight. The splash of water on stone. Lily slipped her dress over her head. She looked so pretty, all white petticoat and camisole. Her legs were muscled, her toes tiny like pearls.

Come, Harley!

I can't.

You can't swim?

No.

I can teach you.

The light from a streetlamp set little fires in her hair.

I can't. But his voice was weak.

Lily laughed and pulled at his pants. Take them off!

And he did, awkward like a boy, pushing each leg down with the other foot.

Your shirt, silly.

Harley pulled his shirt over his head without unbuttoning. He felt Lily staring at the hollowness of his chest; he was a much smaller man without clothes. He put one foot in the river. The current stroked and pulled on his ankles as if the water was alive: Mavis mocking him. He mashed his palms into his eyes.

Lily pranced in the shallows, taunting Harley. She splashed him. He shuddered at the water's smack. She came closer and splashed him again, soaking his underclothes, his legs.

Stop, he whispered.

It's only water, she said. And she kicked a spray that hit his face.

Harley grabbed her forearm. She spun toward him and pushed her body against his. He was paralyzed, by the water, by this girl whose breasts were wet against his chest. His hands, confused and stilled for once, clung to her. Lily pulled his head down so that they were eye to eye. With her other hand, she unbuttoned her camisole.

Harley wanted to swallow her, to split open his skin and take her inside his chest. He led her out of the river and lowered her to the ground. She wrapped her arms and legs around his back, and he poured himself into loving her—salt, sweat, and sinew—but he couldn't, he couldn't. And she nudged him off her and lay next to him petting him like a cat and said, it's alright, it's okay, we'll try again sometime.

The tongue, not the mind, remembers. And because of this, the taste of lake water never leaves Harley's tongue. Its iron bite, its rotten meat of snail, its brightness of green seaweed lives there and lends its tang to any cherry pie or stew he's ever tasted. To every kiss. Over Lily's shoulder, Mavis smiled, not unkindly. Harley felt her sadness, like his, bittersweet. *Haven't we had enough of each other?*

The river rippled with a sudden wind. The drops came lightly at first, then accelerated into a downpour. Harley and Lily ran through the rain back to where Remy was sitting in the Ford, smoking. Lily climbed in without a word.

Harley couldn't find sleep that night. His hands were on fire with agitation, a thousand flies wild with the heat. A muffled knocking kept him awake: a moth beating itself against the window. He lay on his useless quilt, sweating and waiting for dawn. Around five, something shifted in the air. The moth stilled; the birds went mute. He heard men's voices, a dozen or more. The voices came closer, too many to make out individual words. Harley crept to the front corner of the shop where he could spy a sliver of the path outside. The men surrounded the shed. He heard a laugh, short and mean. A joke. He pressed himself against the wall to hide. He smelled gasoline, heard the men cheer, and to his horror, saw bright flames reflected in the polished granite slabs in the shop. The fire spewed black smoke that soon filled the shop and clogged his nose and throat until his breath felt solid, forced in and out like he was pinned underwater. Harley crept along the floor to the front door, opened it. The first kick knocked his head back. Another landed between his legs. White-hooded men dragged him outside and beat him with fists and feet until his body went limp on the ground and the men stopped and ran off, hollering words back at him he couldn't understand. He had blood in his mouth and vomit in his throat. Harley's nose was full of dirt, his eyes swollen, his ribs surely cracked. The fire in the woodshed raged, glass bottles shattering in the heat, the flames feeding on whiskey. But

Harley could do nothing to save it. His head was filled with batting and his muscles twitched. Sounds filtered in as he took a quivering breath: the town clock chiming a quarter hour, the bell summoning the volunteer fire department. To the east, the rising sun pinked the underbelly of clouds.

Bonn came out at noon. A quick look satisfied him that Harley had taken a good beating all around; his nose had swollen up twice its size and one eye was purpley-green. Bonn looked at him with a mix of pity and disgust.

Looks like you got a good once over, Tuttle. Bonn assessed his property. The woodshed was destroyed of course, but he knew it would be. There was no real damage to the shop—he'd been promised there wouldn't be—but it smelled like hell. He shook his head. Your nose, Tuttle.

Harley touched a knuckle to his nostril to stop the blood. Bonn handed him his handkerchief. A boy from town saw a black Ford parked here last Tuesday night about eleven, Bonn said. We all know what that's about. You had to figure someone would find out in a town this size. You stupid?

I'll clean it up, Harley said.

Damn right. And I want you out of here tomorrow. You made me look like a fool, Tuttle.

Bonn glared at the gritty shop, the battered tools, the handful of dead daisies in a vase. The Sears catalogue sold grave markers that were cheaper and easier than anything Bonn could offer. Maybe it was time, he thought, to get rid of this stone business.

I am sorry, Mr. Bonn.

Sorry means nothing to me, Tuttle. This is a town full of good people. I thought you were one of them.

Harley left on the first train the next morning. He heard talk that the Klan had piled stones in the middle of the road leading from Tug Hill and pipe-bombed a black Ford. No one could tell him if it was Remy and Lily inside.

Harley had worked out by now that it wasn't an uncaring God that let the bad happen. It was a distracted one; Harley was pretty much on his own. And he knew at last what he had to do. With his hands he had taken Mavis Staunch's life and with his back he had broken the law. It was with his hands and back he had sinned and it was with his hands and back he had to pay.

He rode the train south to Rochester, then took a bus east. Used money he'd saved bootlegging and bought land not more than a mile from where Mavis Staunch's maple forest once stood. He pitched a campsite and began to use up his body.

He cleared a small patch of land. He levered rocks from the dirt, rolled them onto a tarp, dragged the tarp to the clearing and hoisted them into place to build a foundation. Strained his back and thighs with every load. Smashed a thumb; it never healed. He worked through the winter when he couldn't feel his feet, through the summer when the soles of his boots wore away and his callouses blackened. His sister, Annalee, lived less than three miles away and would try to bring him food, but Harley ate very little. When the walls were knee-high, he still had full use of both arms and legs. By the time they were waist high there was a pain throbbing in his spine that wouldn't let him sleep except on his side. When he got the walls head high, he couldn't use one arm. Harley hired a young Mennonite man to help, and he worked his other arm senseless hammering roof shingles. It took him nearly three years, but he finished the stone house. It was solid like sureness is solid. He'd buried his pain and guilt in the rock and built something good on top of it. This house would stand for decades, maybe even centuries. Where his tombstones had been of use to the dead, this stone would be of use to the living. He'd give the house to people who needed it.

The last thing he did was carve the name "Tuttle" on a piece of oak and nail it above the door. Mavis seemed to approve, as she'd been largely silent these many months, surfacing only occasionally as a reminder of who he no longer was.

Early on an April morning, steam rose from ferns like fog. Harley strapped on his rucksack and padlocked the house. His eyes weren't good and what he saw was never solid, but more a thickness of gnats. Even so, he could make out squirrels chasing each other in the trees. Beyond the woods, on the dirt path leading to the house, more movement. He squinted. What was it? He thought he saw a young woman and a child picking their way through the brambles. Harley blinked; they disappeared. Was he asleep? Dead? His chest rose and fell, and he could feel the sun on his shoulders. He was alive, and for the first time in a long while he felt at peace. Harley unfolded his glasses. It wasn't a woman in the woods, of course, it was a doe and her fawn, unaware of their own beauty, their grace.

Harley walked the three miles to his sister's apartment. The hills that sloped down to Okisee stretched out before him like soft, warm arms; green grasses cleansed the air. He could see the lake through the trees, a gash of blue.

The bed at his sister's house was warm and soft, and Harley was broken. The first night there, he drifted away to the sound of the lake lapping against the shore and the smell of water and weeds and fish, and when she came to him, he lifted the covers to let Mavis into the warmth, which was only fair, and he slept, for what seemed like months.

He woke slowly to a world he'd forgotten. Smell and touch came back first. Vanilla skin on cold pudding. The burnt end of a fresh bread. Skunk cabbage in early spring, unfurling its purple. Feel of nightcrawler squirming under the dirt, smell of mud drying in a cellar, woody heat coming off the bark of an elm. Harley had become porous from three years of living hard; a rain could turn him to paste. His sister, Annalee, told him she thought he had become softer, that his face was more open. He didn't know about that. It had been seventeen years since he'd left Kinder Falls—he'd gone during a cicada summer and returned during a cicada summer, when all the predators were full-up and too sleepy to hunt.

Are you comfortable, Uncle Harley?

Annalee's daughter, Dorie, moved his dead shoulder on the pillow and straightened his legs under the quilt. Pain shot through his spine like liquid knives. People in this house were always moving him around. Giving him laudanum to dull the light and blunt the pain. Harley heard his own voice, but he didn't think he was talking. The girl patted his hand. No one's out in the lake, Uncle Harley. All our people are buried proper in the cemetery on the hill.

He turned his back to her. What did she know. His sister's daughter was a chippy. She was too old not to be married, twenty-eight, and fat. Most single girls were getting jobs in the new car dealership over in Denton. Seemed like everyone had their own car these days. Harley turned on his back and sparks exploded in his bowels.

First light. Harley knew something was different in the house.

Go on in, he's awake, he heard the chippy, Dorie, say.

Harley felt her before he saw her, smelled her. Cloves. The flesh raised on his arms. He opened his eyes and watched her take off her coat; careless with it, dropped it on a chair. Unpinned her felt hat. Her hair, the color of cherry wood in firelight, tangled and reaching all the way down her back.

The heart-shaped face, the slope of her cheek. She was pale, though, or maybe it was the lightless afternoon that made it seem so. Her gloves were violet, and she pulled them off with her teeth as she crossed the room to his bed.

Lily? Harley's voice was a thin, whispery thing. The room was its usual eighty degrees with the heat of the potbelly, but somehow, he was cold.

Yes, it's me. You're shivering, Harley.

I'm always cold.

You must be cold, she'd said that first night. You're shaking.

Lily wrapped both her hands around his. He kissed them. He heard her smile.

She lay down in his bed and curled her body around his. He pressed his boney back into her breasts and belly. She breathed warm air onto the nape of his neck. There was a pleasurable snuffle of snot in his nose. His back relaxed.

We can try again sometime, she'd said.

Three years between her voice then and her voice now, between the river and this room and it was as if only a second had passed. Lily rubbed the thin skin that stretched over Harley's shoulder bone. He felt a twitter of life. A brush of wings from another time.

How did you find me?

She whispered into the back of his neck, warm puffs of clove air. Uncle Remy died. I went for a tombstone. Bonn told me where. The workshop's gone, you know.

The willowy man with the blue-painted nails.

Lily kissed his shoulder. This is where you were a boy?

Yes, a stupid boy, he thought. Stubborn and square-headed. An ordinary boy, fishing with his father. A boy who could have grown up to be someone's husband, someone's father. Can a man forgive a boy who no longer exists? Harley drifted, neither awake nor asleep.

When cleaning a fish, cut the head off first so the eyes don't stare at you.

Chop off the tail so it can't flop out of your hand.

Cut along the belly, gills to tail.

Clean it carefully. Scrape out everything that could tell you what the fish has done and what it ate.

Strip the scales.

There was nothing to it.

A wet, frayed cuff brushed his forehead and Harley sighed in his sleep. *Tell her,* Mavis whispered. He turned to face Lily. It's not that I couldn't swim, Lily. It's not that I didn't love you. I love you.

I know, she said, laughing lightly.

Do you forgive me?

There's nothing to forgive, silly man. Lily rose from the bed and poured a spoonful of laudanum. She held the back of his head. All you need is rest, they say. You swallow this. You'll be good in no time. He opened his lips for her.

When the pain did stop, he had already forgotten it existed. One of his bodies was luxuriating in the world around him, in the silly simplicity of light and scent and warmth. He turned to look out the window. A sudden calm in the lake erased the events of his ten-year-old self and sunlight shot through the pine trees, gilding an old gas can so that it glowed like treasure. He cast his line. Miraculously, he got a tug and the struggle was on. He reeled it in gently, let it out, reeled it, eased it. That's right, boy, that's exactly right, his father said. The trout jumped out of the water and flailed against the hook, but he reeled her in sure and steady and lifted her out of the water by the gills and she shined bright colors in the sun. A rainbow trout shining bright colors in the sunny sun.

Nothing to forgive, she'd said. He heard it right.

My Sixth Toe

Annalee

I had to take him in; he's my brother, what else could I do? For months he lay in bed, barely eating. When I went to check on him, Harley would grab my hand and tell me about the writing crawling across his quilt. He'd describe icy blue mountains out his window. He is a miserable patient, and I am a terrible nurse. He saw people huddled in the corner of his bedroom, chattering. They were real to him; he talked about their bright coats and suspenders. He said there was a robin in the eaves. I could see that the past still snapped at his heels; his legs twitched in his sleep. Do you know any of these people? I'd ask, furious with myself for humoring him.

No. But they won't stop talking.

About what?

I can't tell.

Are they angry?

No, they seem busy, and still at the same time, like they're waiting for the train to go.

Can you see a train?

No, Annalee, I can't.

Are they old people? Men? Women?

All kinds, children too. There's a baby. Do we have anything to give them?

You mean food?

Yes, we should offer them something.

And I, like a fool, would hold out a biscuit to the blank wall, and Harley, satisfied, would sleep, and I would get some peace. It was the French woman, Lily, who cared for him the last few months. Harley's certainly better now, nearly well, and I'm grateful. But last night's storm changed everything.

The wind grew wilder by the hour and the lake roiled and foamed as if it could no longer stand the taste of itself. Come morning, Okisee was the muddy color of a dirty horse blanket, and the beach was littered with debris. The kids found it first. I saw three of them kicking around in the shallows looking for treasure that the waves might've brought in: broken teacups, shards of smoothed glass, silverware. The canoe surprised them. They pulled at it, wet mess it was, slimy with seaweed, and they got a bit of it on the beach. The canvas was partly eaten away but the ribs were intact, so the thing looked like skin stretched over a skeleton. I knew it was Mavis Staunch's canoe. I'll never forgive Harley for giving me that secret to haul through my life like a sixth toe. I saw him do what he did to that canoe, and he saw me watching.

In the afternoon, more kids came by to look. I could hear them talking. Looks like a boat, they said. I tried to think of who would remember that awful night. The Knapps, maybe? The Brouwers would for sure. My heart pounded like crazy as I waited for dark.

The night went gray to charcoal gray; bats stitched the sky. I knew there were eyes everywhere, that I had to work quickly. There was a rowboat beached a few yards down the shore. I shoved it into the water. I waded in, guided the boat over to the canoe, and looped a piece of clothesline from the back of the rowboat to the front ribs of the canoe's corpse. I tugged it into the shallows, then climbed in the rowboat and oared deep into the lake's belly towing the wreckage. When I reached the center, I untied the rope and waited until the canoe slipped into the black. There you go, Mavis. It's yours, you keep it.

Voices. I heard children's voices. I knew that they saw me, silhouetted against the scant light. I knew what they thought, and I didn't do anything to disabuse them. Their parents will tell them it is a trick of the eye, but the children knew better. Mavis Staunch had come to take back her canoe.

You've got to go, I told Harley when I got back to the apartment. Leave before there's trouble. Lily nodded.

It was months before I heard from them and then only a card saying they'd gone north to Galen, on the Clyde River. Good. They're someone else's problem now.

Galen, on the Clyde River

1938

Lily

We were no longer young. We were quilt-puckered from col-larbone to ankle and swollen from ankle to toe from the work we'd done as wives and mothers. We'd dug gardens and wrung laundry with the same hands that cradled stillborn babies. We sang hymns with the same lips that scolded salesmen and lied about what we thought about our husbands. We crimped pies and boiled potatoes and woke every three hours at night, wan-dered our homes in the dark, sighing at the beauty of moon-light threading through fences and across wide swaths of grass and wanting something we couldn't name.

In hindsight, her youth could have been why we were so drawn to her. It was early in the summer—more than two years ago, mid-June, the mosquitos newly born and mad with the heat, the Clyde a stinking trickle. We were curious, of course. The apartment she and the man rented was dead in the middle of Galen next to the Rexall on the first floor, with windows fac-ing the street. We'd stroll by on our business and walk slowly, not looking, but you couldn't help but see the small table close to the window covered with a deep blue cloth and candles burning on it. The pale-yellow curtains, pulled to the side, a lifted veil.

Neither one of them wore a wedding ring, which we

decided was because they were uncle and niece until we saw them arm in arm outside the butcher's shop, looking in at the chickens hanging in the window. The butcher's wife at the counter thought she heard an accent on the woman: Quebecois. Foreigners! We also took note of how he looked at her, and how he touched her lightly on the arm or back as if he didn't believe she was real. We could see that he loved her in a way that our husbands did not love us.

They seemed mismatched: he was worn and deep-lined, stiff and fidgety, and she was small and snaky, although we had to admit, pretty in a china-doll way. Maybe he fought in the Great War, we whispered. Maybe he had been in one of the German camps. Within a week, they had taken in one of the stray dogs that lived by the river.

Then the sign appeared, hand-painted in perfect, curving letters. Madam Lily, Tarot and Palmistry. Underneath that, Medium. We agreed that the business would fail in Galen, of all places. We were a quiet town. Even our waterways were still; you couldn't take a boat down the Clyde for all the dead trees in the way, and the span of the Erie Canal that ran through town was so shallow we liked to say the fish were sunburned.

We were correct, of course. Estelle, who worked across the street at the bank, reported that no customers came or went from the apartment. The humidity of July buckled the paint at the edges of the sign. By August some of the letters had smudged so that the sign read Mad Lil, Tat and Palmy. And didn't it make us laugh to call it that, Tat and Palmy. We couldn't imagine what Mad Lil and himself—Harley was his name—were living on, or feeding that dog, but we came to see that Lil did her shopping in a thick fur coat and hat in all but very hot weather, very extravagant. We wondered if her eyes could change color; even after she'd been living here for a while, none of us could say if they were blue or brown.

One afternoon, an old woman inched down the sidewalk. It wasn't the organist from the Methodist church, although she looked to be that old. Long, dark housedress, thin scarf over her head, bent from the waist like a hay hook, thumping along overdramatically with the help of a cane. We happened to be having rye toast at the Rexall counter and made note of the woman's slow progress and were curious as to where she was headed. When she knocked on the door of Tat and Palmy, our interest grew to a point. When she reappeared after an hour, she seemed to move faster, like a much younger woman. We watched her stop and admire the joe-pye weed, seemingly breathing in the air with great pleasure. We watched until she was out of sight. What, we asked each other, could have happened in there? None of us wanted to be first, but we agreed that someone had to investigate. We elected Evangeline; she had the kindest face.

It had to be the hottest day all summer. When Evangeline disappeared inside Tat and Palmy, we gathered at the Rexall to wait. Fans rifled the paper napkins in their holders. Our slips stuck to our thighs. Finally, she emerged. The apartment is filled with soft yellow light, Evangeline said, the color of buttercups. It's decorated with acorns, shells, colored pebbles, dried violets, bleached bones. The whole apartment, she said, in a tone of unnerving reverence, is a shrine to all the beauty that is around us that we never see. Evangeline said that when she walked in, she felt an ache of a joy so large she couldn't comprehend it, as if Mad Lil and Harley had gathered up the sunshine and filled their house with it. Because of the yellow curtains, Evangeline said, people out on the street look like saints, haloed in sun. Evangeline does not normally speak like this.

Was the man there? we asked; we hadn't seen him in weeks. Is it clean? How many rooms do they have? Are there weapons? We took Evangeline's hands and turned them up to examine her palms. What did she tell you?

Evangeline's forehead creased. She said I should keep Tad home tomorrow because there will be a motor accident and he might be hurt. We started to cluck our tongues, but Evangeline gave us such a sharp look we stopped. The Rexall fans were simply pushing hot air around, and several of us said they could feel a headache coming on. We went back to our own kitchens to berate our husbands and wash our grandchildren with harsh soap. We had more questions now than answers.

Evangeline did keep her son Tad home the next day. We studied the local paper for news of an accident and found only one—a bread delivery truck and a bicycle—but it was nowhere near where Tad could have been. There was no talking to Evangeline about it; she brought a yellow cake to Tat and Palmy as a thank you.

Other women began visiting Mad Lil over the next months; mostly the younger ones, first-time mothers who fussed about fevers and children who couldn't read. Mad Lil told the Williams girl to keep her baby away from the cat and she did. Lord knows what would have happened, the Williams girl gasped as she held her seven-month-old like the baby was made of glass. Mad Lil told another mother to replace the chain on her son's bicycle, and of course she did. If she hadn't, she believed, her eight-year-old would have ridden too fast down the hill and onto the tracks where he'd be stuck by the Erie express. Mad Lil drew circles with a lead pencil on the soles of the shoes of the banker's daughter to attract a lover. She threw stones into the Clyde at the new moon and counted the rings to see how many children the sloe-eyed waitress, Clara, would have.

Eventually, we all went. Those of us with migraines, those losing their sight, those with nasty-tempered children or bad husbands, all slipped through the door to Tat and Palmy to whisper with Mad Lil. We began to believe we had a direct line to the future, and that it was given to us because we were good people, and kind, and deserved to be protected from pain. And we genuinely liked the man, Harley. He was rail-thin and ashen, but always had a kind word. You wouldn't think he'd generate much heat, but when he touched your shoulder to say hello, his hand was warm.

Things grew stranger the next year. Mad Lil claimed she was being guided to serve others more broadly and that she would hold summer message services in the woods chapel outside town. None of us were Spiritualists, of course. We were fully modern women suspicious of the idea of mediumship, and frankly, unnerved at the prospect of our dead visiting us with advice. What did they know; the dead were us, only slighter. Worst of all, what Mad Lil called an outdoor chapel was an abandoned, dilapidated collection of rough-hewn wooden benches a quarter mile from town.

The woods in summer are damp, breathing spaces. We could smell each other's musk and powder when we sat down on the benches. The pine trees rose all around us and the scent of sap reminded us of the flannel lining of our childhood sleeping bags. The young mothers twittered reverently; they took up the front rows.

Mad Lil stood and smiled at us. A breeze ebbed, as if waiting to hear. The earth is tattooed, Mad Lil began, in that quiet, accented voice. We've scratched furrows into its surface and filled them with color: corn, grapes, soy, wheat. These are our marks, the record of what we've done, how we've lived, what we care about. But there is another world beyond this one. It is an unmarked world, the world of spirit, and we enter it through death. All our loves are there, waiting, within our grasp. Our journey is not a solitary one. Invisible hands guide and protect us.

Her skin was translucent. Mad Lil walked toward one of the young mothers. I have someone with me. May I come to you? The woman nodded. I have James with me. Did you have a James in your life? Yes, yes, the woman said. James is here and he wants you to know that it's all right about the house. Does that make sense to you? The young woman blushed a deep red. "May I come to you?" Mad Lil asked the Gooley sisters, both dark-haired and twitchy. I have two men, walking together. Brothers? They're proud of you, they want you to know that. Do you understand? The sisters sighed and slumped against each other. Smiling widely, they put several dollars into Lil's collection basket on their way out.

When we stepped back into the incarnate world outside the chapel, we were newly aware of a cacophony: crickets in the grasses, sparrows flushed from blackberry bushes, tractor engines, the ever-present scold of mockingbirds. It made us feel small in a way we couldn't describe.

It's lovely, don't you think, Evangeline said quietly, the idea of being held by invisible hands?

Again, Evangeline does not normally speak like this.

Stranger still, the bank teller, Estelle, chimed in: I heard that when a Canadian lumberman shoots a deer, he wraps himself in the skin to ward off witches.

The rest of us kept our thoughts to ourselves.

And so it went, the meetings and the messages, until it grew too cold and Mad Lil added private medium sessions to her Tat and Palmy offerings.

Through Mad Lil, the woman in a green velvet cloak with a blue feather came again and again to the Estelle and let her know that she should urge her husband to take the second job he was thinking about. Estelle was moved to do this, and was the happier for it, with her husband gone from the house many more hours every day and extra money coming in. She booked a weekly time at the Tat and Palmy with Mad Lil as breezily as she would a hair appointment. Margaret, the postmistress, heard from a dead aunt that Margaret's son was destined for the air force, and Margaret went home right away and urged her son to enlist, seeing that there were no major wars and he was not interested in getting a regular job. When he did, she turned the overstuffed chair he always sat in toward the window so she could sit peacefully and watch the grackles swarm her yard, pecking their iridescent heads at the grass. She, too, saw Mad Lil regularly.

The spirits warned us that the muck-throttled Clyde River would swell in late autumn rain, and surely it did. When a carelessness set the Frost Hill farm on fire and the flames spread to the fields around it, we knew it would not reach us, and we did nothing to protect ourselves because we knew we didn't have to. The flames didn't jump the town line, and we were smug about that. Mad Lil had given us the confidence of knowing.

But then came the snow. It began falling on Christmas, and we swooned to see it blanketing the town like a postal card. Our hearts were full. But it continued snowing, silently, steadily, one foot, two feet, more. Our cars were buried, some on the side of the road where we'd had to abandon them. Estelle's husband was forced to walk more than a mile home from his night job and the poor man suffered a heart attack at the end of his driveway. No ambulance could get through the snowy streets; he died there. The coal truck couldn't get through either, and people who hadn't put in enough wood were left to freeze in their homes. We lost a high school math teacher and his wife. Ploughs shoved piles of snow into mountains that reached past the first story of the Grange. Tree branches poked through snow crust like the fingers of a drowning man. Our windows were covered by drifts, our doors blocked, our mailboxes submerged beneath the snow.

After three days, it stopped. Estelle buried her husband and went to work as a chambermaid at the Holiday Inn in Lyons. The seniors graduated without Algebra II, and we had snow on the ground until July. Most shockingly, Margaret's son went down in a plane during training exercises over the Yellow Sea.

Why hadn't Mad Lil warned us? We were furious.

We gathered in our kitchens and went over the facts, the sequence of tragedies. Would Estelle be a widow if it wasn't for Mad Lil? Would Margaret's son be alive? The math teacher? We began to recall several oddities that occurred after Mad Lil came to Galen. Sudden nosebleeds. Dead fish in the Clyde. And the birds. We'd never seen so many mockingbirds gathered along the telephone wires as we did that spring, squawking at us whenever we left our houses. Hundreds of them, shrill and punishing. We'd wave our arms and they'd take off, a dark cloud, but then they'd resettle on a roof and continue to berate us. Worst of all was this: now that she knew so much about us—what we were afraid of, the things we wished for, things we'd said about our sisters-in-law and our husbands, all that we hid in our palms and cards, all that we'd confessed on those benches in the woods—could she use it against us? If Mad Lil could protect us, we reasoned, she could also harm us.

The young mothers stopped making appointments with Mad Lil and kept their children close when she was near. We said the Our Father when we had to pass by the Tat and Palmy. We did not speak to Mad Lil when we met her in the market. A second winter passed.

In March of '38 we heard that Mad Lil's Harley had died. We kept up our distance. We had our own dead, and we were sick of funerals. Let her be, we told each other. Let her keep company with her own dead, not ours. Evangeline told us Mad Lil planned to bury Harley up on the hill where Estelle's husband was, and Margaret's son, the math teacher and his wife, our own parents. We wondered, as we often did, where her people were. Or his. Why couldn't she put him with his people? There's a sister in Kinder Falls, Evangeline said, but Mad Lil didn't want him buried there.

For weeks Mad Lil only came out of her apartment at dusk, and when she did, she headed for the woods, eyes straight ahead. She was thin, hardly there, and wore the fur coat and hat no matter what the temperature. We'd peek in the windows of the Tat and Palmy when she was gone; the whole apartment looked as gray as four o'clock in the morning.

Come May, Mad Lil sent word to the young mothers she would start her chapel meetings again; that her Harley had come and asked her to do it.

The audacity.

We talked, we met. We were in agreement.

Come meeting day we arranged ourselves in the front rows and waited while others, all the younger women, tentatively filed in. We turned to eye them. Carp, they were. Useless fish who nibble stupidly on the rubber boots that sink to the bottom of a lake because you never know; it could be food.

Mad Lil stood at the front of the chapel and looked everyone in the eyes. We, of course, wore our sunglasses, as shots of noontime sun speared through the trees and made us squint. Forgiveness is what frees you, she began in that lilting, accented voice. This is what Spirit teaches, this is what Spirit knows. Forgiveness is love.

The gumption.

Mad Lil turned to us. Her voice was quiet. I have a woman with me: Mary? Mabel? We all shook our heads, no. She tried again. There's a woman in a hat with an iridescent bluebird feather stuck in it; she's wearing a green velvet cloak and she wants to tell you something about a well. We knew that was Estelle's person, but we shrugged our shoulders and stared at Mad Lil stonily. I'm afraid I don't recognize who you are describing, we each said as she came to us. Mad Lil gave us a baffled look. Margaret, who'd lost her son, rolled her eyes, stood up and called it all nonsense. One of the young mothers in the back row burst into tears and ran from the chapel. Evangeline leapt to her feet and held up her hands. My hands, she croaked, look at how ugly they are! I'm afraid to touch them together!

We pulled her down to the bench and shushed her.

Spirit has its own logic, Mad Lil said, but her voice faltered, and she ended the meeting. We left her there standing among the trees by herself. People always think they want to know the future, but ultimately, it is unhelpful.

Evangeline was quiet all the way home. Finally, she spoke. It's all sticks made of nothing, she said. We didn't know what to make of that so we let it be.

The Tat and Palmy sign disappeared. The new postmistress reported that several boxes of belongings were sent to Canada. It was Evangeline who saw Mad Lil last. She was out on her back porch when Mad Lil walked by in her big fur coat and hat. We'd had a cold rain the night before, and Evangeline, for no good reason, put on her coat and boots and followed Mad Lil into the fields and down the path to the woods chapel, where she expected Lil to sit and wait for word from her Harley, which, as was perfectly clear to all of us, was not coming. No, Evangeline said, she did not do that. She said that Mad Lil stood at the front of the chapel, lifted her face to the sky and opened her mouth. It was inhuman, Evangeline said, the sound that came out, as if she was vomiting the madness and rage of every soul on earth. Mad Lil shook with such violence,

Evangeline said, that her body nearly lifted off the ground. She screamed louder and louder and louder until at last nothing came out of her mouth and the woods were silent. Then, Evangeline said, Mad Lil left the chapel, walking faster and faster, until she was loping, running, galloping, and all Evangeline could see was a brown ball of fur disappearing among the black trees, a blur of movement that could have been Mad Lil, or a deer, or a trick of the late afternoon light reflecting off the wet leaves. Evangeline followed her until she vanished.

Evangeline knew, she said, that Mad Lil was gone for good because Mad Lil's dog was sitting on Evangeline's porch when she returned. When Evangeline opened the front door, it walked right inside, jumped on her sofa and curled up. Evangeline phoned down to Harley's sister, Annalee, in Kinder Falls, to see if she wanted the dog but Annalee said she was about to head south and couldn't bring a damn dog. Evangeline liked the dog well enough, so she kept him. Named him Spirit.

The rain came hard that whole week, a rain so strong you heard a brass band in the way it echoed against hard surfaces. The Clyde swelled up and swallowed its banks. Our lawns flooded, sewers backed up, drains overflowed. When the rains stopped at last, our basements were covered in a sticky sludge that never quite came clean.

A young couple moved to town and turned Tat and Palmy into a jumble shop. We enjoyed looking through the shelves of leaded glass, old linens, wedding veils, Tinker Toys. We tried to describe how the place looked before—the stones, bones, flowers, and shells; the little table with the deep blue cloth— but we couldn't agree.

We remember what we choose to remember, Evangeline said quietly.

We told the new young couple about Mad Lil's furs, and Harley, and how we came to that apartment to wash the body when he passed. How we embraced Lil and sat with her. How we brought our salads and lemonade, and how she drank up our kindness. We'd pick up a teapot or a china butter dish— how much for this?—and smile at each other remembering how good we'd been to her. She was probably back with her own people now, we said, and although we didn't know where that was, we all agreed it was the best place for her.

2

STAYING BIRDS,
LEAVING BIRDS

Those who kept birds in cages noticed a dusk-time fluttering of wings against the cage wall in late October, what German scientists named *zugunruhe*: nocturnal migratory restlessness. For most of the caged birds this restlessness seemed to pass, and they blissfully ignored the red-tailed hawks, warblers, and thrushes riding the wind above Kinder Falls. The caged birds were staying birds, by circumstance rather than choice. They were more akin to the cardinals, chickadees, and pileated woodpeckers, to the sober crows, juncos, nuthatches, and jays, all of the staying birds who dug in for the winter, albeit with grim determination and streaky plumage. They had to. Otherwise, who would sing?

But the leaving birds! Broad-winged hawks headed for Argentina, wood thrushes on their way to Veracruz, bald eagles to Fort Myers, yellow warblers to the Gulf of Mexico, goshawks to Tennessee! No frozen fields, no ice, no bitter berries for them! Swooping and banking overhead, the leaving birds caught a southerly draft over Okisee and rode it until the lake was nothing more than a tiny sparkle, a wink, something stuck in their memory as important, but not as important as leaving.

Red Sails in the Sunset

1938

Annalee

The last thing Annalee wanted was Harley's damn dog. The last thing she needed was something else to take care of. She'd done her time. She'd raised her daughter Dorie, tended to her brother Harley, God rest his soul, waked and buried her parents, all the while being a good citizen of terminally tranquil Kinder Falls. Tonight, at ten o'clock, her real life would begin. Mr. Knox would turn onto her street in his 1938 Ford V8, and she'd get in. They'd smile all the way to Florida. He had a friend in Jacksonville who could set them up in an apartment. She'd learn to drive, they'd buy a new car, just for her, one where the top rolled down and you could feel the wind rush past your ears like a jet engine.

She had taken special care dressing this afternoon; her clothes needed to stay fresh for a day and night, maybe longer. Her skirt was pale blue, light wool, straight to her mid-calf. Her blouse was three-button rose-blush silk with a tiny bow at the throat, her earrings and necklace, pearl. Or looked like. Her stockings—an extraordinary gift from a lonely salesman she'd kept company one night at the Lamplighter—were wrapped in tissue. Annalee unfolded the paper rapturously, smoothing the folds until the shining, sun-golden fabric was exposed. She gathered a stocking and dipped her toe in, smoothing it up the leg, tugging gently, until it met the garter. She slid the darker hem over the clasp and secured it. Perfect, she thought. Then the other. She admired herself in the mirror. Annalee had a certain unique style, cleverly cobbled together with zippers torn from old clothes and the ends of bolts from the Singer store where she worked until it closed, like all the others. And she had a few years left; she was barely fifty. Static electricity sparked off the silk of her slip where it met her nylons as she walked. Her charm bracelet tinkled: a clock, tiny scissors, fish, baby bottle, high heel, sewing machine. Her life in miniature.

She walked to the town hall to pick up a copy of her birth certificate, which she'd need if she wanted to prove she was American; whatever few jobs there were went solely to Americans these days. And, Annalee thought, she'd need it if she ever wanted to apply for a marriage license. If. The sound of her heels clicking down the tile corridor made her feel she was a woman of importance, always did. It thrilled her. Her daughter's childhood friend, Frances Price, worked in the Clerk's Office; a too-serious young woman with the face of a Great Dane. Frances had sense, though, unlike Annalee's own daughter, Dorie, who'd forgotten to wear a slip under her dress at her own wedding and told everyone, giggling and blushing, making it worse. Now Dorie was about to have a baby. At thirty-two, too old, in Annalee's opinion, and Annalee felt far too young to be called Grandma. She needed to leave Kinder Falls before she was asked to help out.

Frances smiled at Annalee and handed her an official-looking envelope.

Annalee put the certificate in her purse. Plans for the weekend? she asked, to be polite.

Mother's, Frances said cheerfully.

Sounds lovely. Take good care. Annalee smiled at Frances. Such a serious face.

During the day, during her mother hours, Annalee had stayed backstage, moving curtains and arranging props where no one would see her or ask more of her than was required for the job. But after hours, after her daughter was asleep, she put on eyeshadow and drew a line up the back of her calves, stood on her toes and looked at her legs in a mirror. The legs were good but try as she did to stretch her spine and neck, she was square from shoulders to hips. Her hair was colorless; faded brown going gray. Her best weapons were her eyes, her Claudette Colbert eyes.

Annalee could fill her movie star eyes with a combination of longing and aloofness that usually brought men to her, curious. She'd perch at a table by the window in the Lamplighter Inn, don a pair of dark movie star sunglasses and smile out at the sidewalk as if she was enjoying the drama on the street. Then she'd remove her sunglasses, cup her cheek in manicured fingers, and fix her mascara-ed eyes on a man sitting alone at the bar. Usually she could make him turn, and if he did turn, she'd giggle and act surprised to be caught. She'd raise an eyebrow, and he'd come over to the table with some excuse: you look like you know this town, can I ask you a question? It looks like your glass is empty, may I buy you another? I don't see why not, she'd purr. They'd never get very far with her, as she was simply rehearsing. When the right man came down the pike, she'd be ready. And he had come. He had a car, which cost $500. She knew that because that was the first thing he said to her.

I see you looking out at my car, there. It's a brand new 1938 Ford V8. $500 car. Your glass is empty. Can I buy you another?

I don't see why not.

Bill Knox. He extended a hand. The fingernails were clean and buffed. You're a very beautiful woman.

She took it. Annalee Tuttle. You're a magnificent liar.

And he pulled a chair close to her, nodded to the bartender to bring drinks. Knox was shorter than her, Annalee noted, but movie star men were often short too. I'm going to entertain you with a story you're not going to believe, he said, but it's true.

I'd believe anything, she said.

Okay then. The bourbon that arrived smelled expensive.

There was a guy, Joseph, ran a grocery, you know?

Bill Knox's lips were shapely. Annalee concentrated on them and murmured encouragement.

Fruit mostly. And one day this stranger comes in and pulls out a gun and tells Joseph if he doesn't come up with $2,000, he's going to shoot him. $2,000! So Joseph, he's real upset— figures it's a rival fruit business guy—he tells his friend Leo and Leo says, you don't have to take that. I know a guy over in Albany. Knox paused to take a long drink. You following?

Annalee's eyes blinked slowly. She sipped her old-fashioned.

So Joseph and Leo, they go see this guy in Albany. Here's where it gets crazy. The guy says, yeah, I know that goon who's bothering you. Come with me. They all get in a car and go to this place, a restaurant. You're not going to believe what happens next.

Try me, Annalee said, smiling.

Ok. There's a front room and a back room. The Albany guy goes into the back room. And bang, bang, two shots, loud and sharp as hell.

Annalee widened her eyes. She leaned forward and cupped her chin in her palm.

Joseph runs into the back room and sees the guy who threatened him on the floor, covered in blood. Joseph is shaking, so Leo gets him in the car and they all get out of there fast.

And did they get away? Annalee asked, her voice bourbon-soft.

Well, yeah. But they had to find someone to get rid of the body and in the end, poor Joseph ends up having to pay a couple of knuckleheads to do it.

Annalee pressed a delicate finger on Knox's forearm and waited for a reaction. He stopped talking. She smiled. How much money? she asked.

He owes, like, $1,000 to these guys. So Joseph, he empties out all the money he has, which is only $600, and gives it to his friend Leo to take to the knuckleheads. Bet you can see how this ends, can't you?

Annalee shook her head slowly, eyes fixed on Knox. I can't begin to imagine.

Knox laughed, loud and long. The other people at the Lamplighter turned their chairs to look at him. He raised his arms in triumph. The whole thing is a con! The dead guy is really a guy covered in ketchup. Ketchup! No one got shot and Leo masterminded the whole thing to get Joseph's money. His friend Leo!

Well, I never, Annalee purred. She relaxed back in her chair. She didn't believe the story for a second.

Knox signaled for another round. Annalee smiled to herself. He lit a cigarette, offered her one. She took it.

The Ketchup Murders, she murmured.

Yep, he said. A complete con. Then again, you have to hand it to them. It was good theatrics.

This was her guy. Annalee had known it the moment he turned around on his stool and the light from the window caught the side of his face: Bogart in "Up the River." His voice was a tinge nasal, but he knew how to tell a good story. It didn't take her long to wind herself around him. Only a month. And now they had plans.

She hated Kinder Falls with its lean little shops that sold nothing but housework: buttons, hardware, soaps, brooms.

And now the shop owners couldn't afford to fix their broken awnings. Empty storefronts grew like cancer. Signs swung useless: Coca Cola, Quaker Oil, Nescafe. Everyone moved in with everyone else and lived on top of each other like mice. They drank coffee at the drugstore counter from cups the color of old diapers. They complained on summer evenings on their stoops as they eyed moths butting against lightbulbs, trying to predict the weather from a sky that went from fuchsia to lavender to the color of a bruised eye socket on day three, something not unfamiliar in this town of flat-headed farmers and minor bureaucrats, small-minded men with no ambition.

Florida. The word was like Cherry Coke on her tongue. Once they were settled, she'd send a postcard back and tell Dorie about the orange groves and how the water was so warm you could swim in October. In Florida you didn't have to talk about Hitler and Chamberlain or what Japan was up to in China or Mussolini in Africa. You didn't have to walk past the man who stood outside the First National with a sign hung around his neck that said, "I believed the banks." Only people who lived with the snow and mud of New York State felt the need to be dreary. Winter makes you dull, Annalee thought. It was the lack of light. Florida was sunny all year round.

Annalee got back to her apartment at dusk. She packed the things she wanted to take with her in a small suitcase. Dorie and her slow-but-always-kind Sam would move in before the baby came and make good use of it. Her farewell gift to them: a nice, fully furnished apartment in downtown Kinder Falls. No one could call her a bad mother for that. At the last minute, she remembered the cookies. Knox had asked her to make chocolate chip cookies, and she had a tin of them. She thought it was romantic, like they were married already.

Annalee stood outside her apartment and took a last look around. The air was damp with the smell of plant sex and rot.

Nubs grew on the lilac branches like warts and trees sprouted large, ugly bolls. Her heels sunk in and sucked out of the mud as she walked across the grass. When she stepped on the road, one heel left a smear of dog shit on the tar. She scraped it clean. Checked her face in her compact. The moon hung in the mirror.

Mr. Knox's Ford V8 rolled up at exactly 10 p.m. She smiled into the headlights and picked up her suitcase. He waved at her out the driver's window. She saw his head, his hat, silhouetted. A red ash flared; he was smoking. He slid out of the car and opened the back door for Annalee. She didn't move.

A man was sitting in the passenger seat.

Evening, Sugar Tits, Bill Knox said, smiling. He was staring over her head, cigarette hand balanced on the back door. He jerked his head toward the passenger. We're taking Don Epps here with us, he said. Because of his New England accent, Annalee heard Dawn Epps and it confused her. In fact, everything was suddenly confusing. Annalee remained standing outside the car. Every instinct she had told her something was off.

Knox loaded Annalee's suitcase into the trunk. She stood, erect, holding her purse, waiting for Mr. Epps to move into the back seat so she could slip in next to Knox. Epps sat like a lump of lead, didn't even move his head. Knox closed the trunk and stood beside the car's back door and bowed deeply. In you go, princess. She refused to move. We've got to make time, Dollface. Jump in. Mr. Don Epps stared straight ahead. Annalee searched Knox's eyes for the spark that said, I'm joking, just play along, but there was nothing in them but a badly disguised impatience. With all the dignity she could muster, Annalee climbed in. She felt Knox's eyes on her bottom. She perched gingerly, not wanting to surrender to the Ford's back seat. The soles of her feet burned with tiny blisters from walking in new heels.

Knox eased the car through town and onto the two-lane. The men gazed ahead into the darkness as they rode along 14 going south. It was misting. The fuzzy glow of an oncoming car's headlights caught them for a moment, and Annalee thought they looked like movie actors in their raincoats and with their hats pulled low over their foreheads. Not handsome movie actors, though. Mr. Knox, and she hated to admit it, wouldn't age well. His eyes were already sinking into slits and his skin slid down his face and gathered in jowls. Don Epps, Dawn Epps, the rude stranger, he was going to look like a pie pan until he died. No depth: flat, dull.

Annalee tried to focus on the roads, where they were turning, any landmarks. She'd never been far from Kinder Falls and she didn't drive. She had no idea where they were. Or now, where they were really going. The highway rolled on and on in darkness. She fidgeted, crossed and uncrossed her legs. She couldn't stand the silence. Nice night for a drive, she said. No real rain, anyway. Would have been awful to do this drive in the rain, wouldn't it?

Knox grunted.

Are you related to the Kinder Falls Epps? Annalee asked, as politely as she could. Everyone knew the Epps; the name was synonymous with money and land. People said that even when corn went down to ten cents a bushel and most farmers went bankrupt, the Epps made money: they sold their corn for heat. She also remembered there was something unfortunate about an Epps, something mean and wrong, back when she was a girl.

He's an Epps alright, Knox said. Ancestor founded the town. Grandfather bought up all the land east of the lake, father bought even more. His brother Mitchell still works it, the poor dog. Donny here's not much of a farmer.

Don Epps reached a hand into the back seat, palm up.

Annalee took it and shook it.

No, Doll, Knox said. He wants a cookie.

She opened the tin and put a cookie in the open palm. Epps sighed.

He wants the tin, Knox said.

The whole tin?

The men stared into a set of oncoming headlights, their heads fat bowling pins in hats. Annalee passed the tin to Don Epps. She heard the rustle of wax paper. Knox reached into his coat pocket and removed a flask. He handed it back to her. Annalee figured she'd better take a bit. She didn't have a good feeling.

Then she remembered what she knew about the Epps from years ago. Wasn't it awful, she said, about Angus Epps, jumping off a trestle bridge? Imagine. Dying all alone like that. Body washing into the lake. Truly horrible.

Don Epps chewed.

That was his uncle, Knox said.

Oh, I'm so sorry, Annalee said.

He didn't jump, Don said, chewing.

Annalee heard the wrinkle of waxed paper, the crunch of Don Epps biting into another of her cookies. He was mumbling: cedar grove, vineyard, cedar grove, stone wall.

What? I didn't hear you, Mr. Epps.

That's just Donny. He notices things that repeat. He's a math whizz. And you should thank him for that.

Why? Annalee asked.

We'll need him in Florida.

Annalee could hear Don Epps swallowing. Her stomach twisted at the sound. They were bringing this rude man all the way down the East Coast?

Cat got your tongue? Knox asked. You're quiet all of a sudden.

Annalee tried to keep her voice calm. What skills? She was furious.

He's good at figuring out money.

You worked for a bank, Mr. Epps?

Knox laughed. Epps? Ha. Kind of. He worked for some lenders up in Albany.

Albany. Everything bad seems to come from Albany, Annalee said, disapprovingly.

I did the numbers for Valenti's people, Epps mumbled.

Donny, here, he's a smart guy, Knox said. He took a little off the top of each job he worked. When in Rome, right?

You worked for gangsters? Annalee asked.

The headlights of an oncoming car lit the wet trees on either side of the road. Epps shoved another cookie in his mouth. Back office, he mumbled.

He was the brain guy, Knox said. And now we have him. Epps is the brains, and I'm the salesman. And you—

Me, yes, Mr. Knox, what am I?

You're the sugar on top.

Annalee sighed loudly.

Don't worry, Doll, Knox said. We know what we're doing. He laughed with delight and slapped his thigh. Best idea I've ever heard. Glass-bottom boats! Knox took another drink from the flask, passed it back to Annalee. Yes, glass-bottom boats, baby. Tourism's coming back in that alligator-infested Florida swamp, and we're going to be in on the ground floor. Silver Springs! They made movies there. *Tarzan and His Mate,* you saw it didn't you? They shot that in Silver Springs! Donny's going in half-and-half with a cousin to buy a glass-bottom boat and you and me, we're going to take tourists up and down the Silver River.

Don Epps piped in: People like to see the bottom.

Annalee gripped the flask. Her hand was shaking. The bottom of a river? she said.

Yes. Epps turned to look at her. It's unique.

They rode in silence. Annalee took off her heels and twirled her ankles. Finally she asked, Is the mob buying the boat?

That's the beauty of it, doll. It's all Donny's money. Years of service, years of skimming, years of saving. All in gold.

Don Epps glanced back at Annalee. Gold bars. Thirty of them.

Knox was giddy. And twenty gold coins on top of that!

Twenty-dollar Saint-Gaudens. Double Eagles, .9675 troy, Epps recited.

Annalee huffed. I doubt it, she said. I don't mean to cast aspersions, Mr. Epps, but even if you actually had those gold bars, and I really don't think you do, you know it's illegal without a license.

Epps bit into a cookie. $10,000 fine, ten years in prison, he said, chewing.

Donny's well aware, Knox said. Seems there's a black market for gold that popped up the second everyone had to turn theirs in. And Donny's cousin knows some people.

So where is it?

Silver Springs? It's north of—

No, Annalee said. The gold. Where are you keeping the gold bars?

Plus twenty Golden Eagle coins, Epps reminded her.

She raised her voice. I asked where. It better not be in the car. I don't want to be riding around with contraband. If we get stopped, we could all go to jail.

Knox was grinning. She could hear the wetness of his cheeks against his teeth.

No one will find it. Show her, Donny.

Don Epps lifted a heavy object from beside his feet. He angled an enormous urn over the front seat to Annalee.

See if you can hold it, Doll.

This has got to be thirty pounds! she said, gripping the urn.

Thirty-four pounds, said Epps. It's the bars. The coins don't weigh much.

If anyone asks, if anyone stops us, Knox said, you cradle that thing for dear life. We put ashes on top.

Annalee's hands instinctively flew away from the urn. Dead people's ashes? Who's in there?

Your sister.

I don't have a sister.

That's what you say if anyone stops you, Knox said. Your dear, sweet sister has died, and we are scattering her ashes in Silver Springs, a place she always loved.

Annalee shuddered. Who is it really?

Donny's aunt.

Annalee sat stiffly with the urn beside her; she was afraid to move. It was hideous. Don Epps turned back to her and handed her the empty cookie tin.

She stared at him, dumbfounded.

The gold is underneath the ashes, Knox said. Anyone asks, you hug that urn and cry.

The two men went back to staring at the road ahead. They rode in silence for many miles. The night was getting darker, the clouds inking with coming rain. Annalee stared into the rearview mirror waiting for Knox to look back at her and give her a wink, a smile, anything she could interpret as intimacy, but he was impenetrable. His eyes watched the road, the shadows, the dips and curves.

Annalee spoke at last. I've never seen a dead person's ashes. Can I look?

Whatever you want, Dollface, Knox said.

Annalee removed the top of the urn. She peered into the vessel. In the half-light all she could see were grayish, pebbly grains. She touched them, lightly. And what if I don't go along with this scheme?

Knox and Epps glanced at each other. Long minutes passed. Knox lit a cigarette.

Strangest thing happened in Albany, Knox said at last.

Albany again, Annalee said, disgusted.

Yes, Albany. Guy murdered his girlfriend and stuffed her in a cedar chest.

Don Epps perked up: Wrapped her in a pink striped blanket. She was there for days.

Terrible thing, Knox said. And they were two ordinary people. Maybe even in love.

A passing car lit the men's faces: dark shadows for eyes.

Annalee let a few minutes go by. I did see that in the newspaper, she said. If I remember, they caught the man. She smiled at Knox in the rearview mirror, an innocent smile. And where is he now?

Knox exhaled a long plume of smoke. Attica, probably. Still, he said, gotta hand it to him for the theatrics.

They rode along in the darkness. A half hour later, Knox turned the car off the main road onto a smaller one.

Where are we going? Annalee asked.

Need to stop for bite, Knox said. But he kept driving. The road snaked into thicker and thicker trees so that the darkness became a blackness. Clouds smudged the moon.

I'd like to know where we are going, Annalee said, a bit more forcefully.

Knox ignored her. Don Epps stared straight ahead.

Annalee tried to make out the landscape but all she could see was stand after stand of sumac along the side of the road;

no mailboxes, no light in the distance that might signal a farm-house, no break in the foliage where an access road might lead through a field. They might as well have fallen off the earth.

Well, she said, forcing her voice to sound cheerful. You can tell me at least this, are we in the Catskills or the Poconos?

Knox snorted.

I've always wanted to go back to the Poconos, Annalee went on. Some of my family came from around there. They were Mennonites, actually. Spoke a kind of German at home. I remember visiting their hog farm. The boys laughed at me because I wore my church shoes into the barn. They were good people, though, completely moral people.

There are no completely moral people, Knox said.

No one's completely good, Epps said.

There are definitely good and moral people, Annalee confirmed. No one would know there were bad people if there weren't good people to measure against.

Epps turned his head to look at her. It's good people that are the problem, then, he said.

Knox lit a cigarette. You tell anybody about this trip?

Well of course I did. I told Dorie. To Don Epps she said, my daughter.

Don Epps grunted.

You have children, Mr. Epps?

Epps drummed his fingers on the seat.

It's not easy to raise a daughter, you know, Annalee went on. If it was up to me, I might have left mine on the church steps, and I know that sounds harsh, but it wasn't up to me. I was a teenager when I got pregnant. I was going to marry the boy, but he died before we could do it. He was walking the grain—do you know what that is Mr. Epps—walking the grain? Well, you're in the silo tamping down the grain and you hit an air pocket and it's like quicksand, really. You suffocate. I know you probably

don't hear much about that kind of thing around Albany, but it
happened often enough where I grew up. All I remember about
that boy was that his face was reddish, like he was blushing all
the time. Anyway, before I was even five months along, Daddy
tied our furniture to the bed of a truck and we left home. My
little brother Harley was so mad that he'd have to start a new
school he stopped speaking to me. We moved from Pennsylvania
to Kinder Falls and Mama did most of the raising of Dorie, till
she died and then I picked up, but Dorie was almost grown and
frankly, I don't have the instinct. Oh, I could fake it, like if we
were at a picnic and the other girls had brownies in their lunch
bags and all I had was a few peanuts in my pocket, I could say
look Dorie, peanuts! in such a way that she'd think she was the
Queen of Sheba. You must think I'm awful, but honestly, I don't
have the knack for mothering. Some women don't.

The car turned onto a small road, a service road of some
kind. The tires rode over dried clods of mud. Where are we
going now?

Low, nervous branches brushed the side of the car.

Annalee breathed in slowly through her nose, out on a
count of eight through her mouth. People sometimes thought
we were sisters, my daughter and me. How about that? Sisters.
Annalee could only see the sides of the faces of the two men.
Epps chewed. Knox's jaw twitched. My God, Annalee said, it's
empty out here. Are we lost?

Knox slowed and turned into a parking lot. It was lit in
hazy, misty green. Two gas pumps stood in the dark in front
of a diner, windows bright like a dance hall. A man in dungarees sat outside on a bench at the edge of the lot. Annalee
left the urn on the car seat and walked purposefully into the
diner. Knox joined her at a Formica table in the back corner
and ordered two coffees. Don Epps went to a booth at the other
end to use the payphone.

Knox lit a cigarette and blew the smoke over Annalee's head. He tried to cover her hand with his but she pulled away.

You called me Sugar Tits.

Knox sighed. I'm sorry about that. I'm not usually that kind of guy.

You made me sit in the back seat.

Donny was already in the front.

But you made me sit in the back seat. Like a child. Or a servant.

Or a wife, Knox joked. He glanced at Annalee to see if she knew he was trying to lighten the mood. Oh, come on. Is that why you're mad? Because you had to sit in the back seat?

Annalee smoothed out her skirt. Among many reasons, she said, and stared out the diner window. Honestly. Smuggling gold.

I didn't realize you were such a flower, Knox said.

Annalee's face flushed. I don't think you know this flower very well.

I know her well enough to know I can count on her. Isn't that right? Annalee? Can I count on you? You're with us, right? If we get stopped, if anyone asks?

She stared at her knuckles, wrapped around the handles of her purse.

Knox rolled his eyes and slouched back against his chair. He checked his watch. Midnight. Wonder what's taking Donny, he muttered. He closed his eyes and hummed. Annalee studied the slightly graying spouts of whisker hair that his razor had missed, the red band across his forehead where his hat had been. She felt a sudden affection for him; he hadn't bargained for her.

She dug a nickel from her purse and walked to the jukebox. The first strains of "Red Sails in the Sunset" filled the air. She turned and smiled at Knox, extended her hand. He stood and took it. Annalee put her cool fingers on the back of Knox's neck and he squeezed her tighter. She lifted her cheek to touch his and they swayed back and forth until the music stopped. His palm was warm on her back as he led her back to their seats.

Pretty song, he said.

It is, isn't it.

Guy Lombardo?

Yes. That song always makes me feel happy.

Bright headlights swept the parking lot, and a Greyhound bus edged into the plaza. The man in dungarees stood and dug around in his back pocket.

Annalee watched the scene as she would a movie in the theater: the greenish lighting, the bus, the man in dungarees. She felt like she was a stranger waiting backstage to see what Annalee Tuttle would do. Don Epps was slouched in the phone booth. Knox was blowing smoke up toward the ceiling, a half-smile on his face.

Slowly, she slid her purse over her arm and walked past the phonebooth, out of the diner, across the parking lot and up the steps onto the bus.

Under heavy-lidded eyes, Knox watched her go. He finished his cigarette, dug a dollar bill out of his wallet, and left it on the table. He paused at the door of the diner until the bus pulled out of the plaza and onto the road. Then he went outside.

Annalee watched Mr. Knox grow smaller and smaller, a tiny figure in an aquarium-green-lit world. The bus driver had a bag of pistachio nuts in his lap, and he'd reach down, stick one in his mouth, suck on it for a while, and then spit the shell into a cup. They'd be in Wheeling by dawn, he told her. She bought a ticket and settled back into her seat. She took stock; everything she'd packed for the trip was in the trunk of Knox's car. In her purse she had her wallet, a lipstick, some crackers, a handkerchief, and twenty double Eagles covered in ash, quietly scooped from the horrible urn. She unfolded the handkerchief and rubbed at her hands until they were clean. She picked until the grainy stuff was gone from underneath her fingernails. It wasn't ash at all. More like rough sand from the bottom of Okisee. Glass-bottom boat, my eye, she thought. No one will pay to see the bottom of a river. Annalee settled back into her seat and crossed her legs at the knee. Her nylons were still perfect. A wisp of straw paper skittered across the floor on an invisible breeze. A cloud of diesel warmed her feet. The bus swayed like a cradle.

The man in dungarees came down the aisle and perched on the seat across from her.

Looks like it's just us for a while, he said. Figured I'd introduce myself. I'm Dobbs.

Annalee smiled. Claudette, she said, looking up at him from under her lashes.

Beautiful name, he said.

Ribbons of headlights cut across the man's face as the bus gathered speed. Blue eyes, straight nose, solid jaw. This was a man, she thought, who was exactly who he said he was. In her head she hummed a bit of "Red Sails in the Sunset." She looked up at him with her Claudette Colbert eyes. Yes, she said, I think so too.

Twenty Golden Eagles

Was it Annalee Tuttle or was it Claudette Dobbs who lived more than two decades in Wheeling, West Virginia as the town's most popular driving instructor? Teenage boys were terrified by her flirty personality; teenage girls dressed like her and practiced her laugh. She loved teaching kids how to drive and loved especially being able to work the dual controls from the instructor's side of the car. Wheeling lay in the foothills of the Appalachians and the roads around it were twisty; it took skill to manage them. Every spring she'd go to the town fountain and slip in a gold coin to wish for another accident-free year; every year it worked.

There goes Claudette Dobbs with another victim, people would say when she passed by in the instruction car, her arm out the passenger window, floating like a wing on the wind, such a happy sight. Full stop at every stop sign. Signal right or left a half-block before a turn. But on the straight section of highway south of Woodsdale, she'd let the kids push hard on the gas pedal and go, blood song playing in their ears, hair whipping in the wind, eyes tearing up, until the car's engine shimmied and she had to tap her brakes to bring it back to the speed limit. Just enough to give them a taste of it, she told Dobbs. After which she said, again and again, laughing every time, no children were ever harmed in the training of new drivers in Wheeling.

Prince of Worms

Mitchell

The land around Kinder Falls had lost its red blaze with the clearing of the sugar maples. Few people would remember it, but Mitchell Epps did. Mitchell had watched the town's old families die or move away: the Tuttles, whittled down to the big gal who lived up on the hill, Dorie. The only Staunch left in town was that hard stump of a woman from Ohio, Lucy, who ran a marine gas station off her dock. Even most of Mitchell's own family was gone, starting with his uncle Angus, dead at thirty-two, followed by his grandfather, of old age, and his father last winter of flu, when the temperature went down to thirty-six below and more than one desperate man set his house on fire trying to thaw out the pipes. Mitchell's little brother, Donny, was off in Florida doing God knows what—glass-bottom boats, real estate, amusement park rides—Mitchell had lost track. It was only he and his sister left in Kinder Falls, and she on her high horse all the time because she'd married the banker, Dunn, and lived on the lake with a boathouse and an inboard motorboat. Mitchell was the only one left to manage the sprawling acres his family had amassed over the generations. Mitchell Epps, prince of dung, worms, mosquitos, cows, and flies. God, how he hated farming.

Le Chevalier

1956

Where have you been, Sharon?

The boat dock.

One ear bled a wet trail of pink down her neck. Mitchell followed her to the bathroom. What did you do?

Dad, a little privacy.

Did you think I wouldn't see it?

I *hate* this, she screamed, shoving her full weight against the door to keep him out.

We told you *no*, he said. You were forbidden.

Why do you always make everything into such a big deal?

Who did it? Who pierced your ears? Where? What did you use?

Who cares! And stay out of my room, Dad. I don't want you in there going through my stuff.

I don't go through your stuff.

You stole cigarettes out of my room.

So now you smoke?

Sharon banged out of the bathroom.

Where are you going?

The front door slammed. Mitchell followed Sharon to the front porch and threw a pack of Winstons at her feet.

Sharon turned and looked at him. She smiled a nervy, snide smile. It seemed to Mitchell Epps that his daughter had swallowed the devil whole on her fifteenth birthday. Broken DNA. Snake blood in it. Something.

Thought you didn't go through my stuff, she said.

Nine o'clock, Sharon—

There was the sound of boys hooting and a car radio blasting Elvis, "Heartbreak Hotel," then the squeal of tires and she was gone.

Mitchell's wife wouldn't look at him over supper. Finally, Carol spoke. You do this. You drive her away.

I'm trying to keep her safe, for God's sake. Mitchell took his napkin from his lap and folded it carefully. She's fifteen.

She's a mature fifteen.

Do you really think she's mature? he asked his wife. Honestly, do you trust her?

Carol sighed. I don't want to fight with her. I'm tired of fighting with her.

Sharon had worn them both out. She was a colicky baby who grew into a sneaky, mean child. When she was seven, she drowned a mouse in a jar of Kool-Aid in front of a group of younger children on the school playground. Carol sent her to bed without supper and went to the rectory to talk with the minister. Mitchell sat in the hallway outside Sharon's door and wept. He would just have to love her harder, he thought.

Nine o'clock came and went; Sharon wasn't home. Not home by midnight either. Mitchell and Carol lay awake in bed, each pretending they were asleep. When Carol's breathing at last grew deep, Mitchell went to sit by the bay window that overlooked the town. Here, he would wait for his daughter to come home, as he always did, no matter when that was. He spied a pickup stopped at a red light on Water Street and

Mitchell recognized it as Marty West's. Go home to your wife, Marty, he said to himself; it's after midnight.

The town of Kinder Falls hadn't changed all that much since Mitchell was a boy. More parking lots, sure, and recently, public ash trays. There was a McDonald's where Hector's Notions had been, a Sears, and for a reason no one could understand, a small theatrical company renting out the basement of St. Andrews Episcopal church. For all that, it was still a small town. He knew Sharon chafed at the smallness, the grinding repetition of their lives. He did too. Things only grow as big as the container they are planted in.

Sharon came in well after midnight. Mitchell snuck back to bed before she saw him.

Turned out the theatrical company had done summer stock in the Catskills for years but came to Kinder Falls to launch a permanent, year-round theater on the lake. Carol heard that the players were quite good, which is how Mitchell found himself in an uncomfortable metal folding chair in the church basement waiting, with forty-odd neighbors, for *Come Back Little Sheba* to begin. He'd never seen a live play before and he wondered how long they took. He cracked his knuckles. Carol glared at him. The basement got dark, the stage lights faded up, the actors took the stage, and Mitchell's jaw fell open.

It was voyeuristic, watching the performers without them seeing him. He knew their secrets in less than two hours: the wife lost a baby, the husband was drinking again. It tore his heart out thinking about the lives they could have had, how they hated what they'd done to each other and themselves. He wept for the dog, Sheba, who he knew would never come home. These people could not escape themselves; it was devastating. Although he knew it was an illusion—the scenery was painted, the actors pretending—it felt more real than his own life. When the performers took their bows, Mitchell stood with all the others and clapped loudly. Carol stared at him, aghast. Sit down, she hissed.

Mitchell signed up to volunteer for the Pleasant Valley Players that night. He was in awe of the whole idea of acting; that you could slide another body over your own and give it life. Each time he entered the basement of St. Andrews it was with reverence, as if he was going to Sunday service. He watched every show from backstage, transfixed by the way the stage light leaked into the wings and illuminated great swirls of dust mites. He did all the jobs the theater needed: he set up chairs, repaired props, ironed costumes, replaced makeup brushes and pots, anything, and for these small gestures he was appreciated and welcomed as an important member of the group. At the closing night cast party for *On the Town,* Mitchell wore Hildy's sequined butterfly clip as a joke and sang a few bars of "You're Awful." The actors all laughed and toasted him. To Mitch! they shouted, Bravo!

The next morning he was overcome with cold, debilitating shame.

What's wrong with you? Carol asked. You look awful.

He smiled at her. Nothing. Bad dream. He shook his head.

Carol looked over her glasses at him for a long moment. I don't mind, you know.

Don't mind what?

Whatever you're up to at the theater. I don't mind it. Don't even care, as long as you leave it there, and don't bring it home.

What are you talking about?

You know, theater stuff. Actors. They have airs.

I'm not going to get airs, Carol. I'm a farmer.

Just don't go wearing an ascot or buying a pink shirt. We are regular people, ordinary people.

Mitchell thought about how easily the actors stripped their costumes off after a show, how comfortable they were in their bodies. How they all hugged each other before they went onstage. How they talked about themselves constantly, their hair, their lovers, their diets. They were different for sure.

The boys coming around for Sharon were getting older. Mitchell didn't recognize them with their slicked back hair and leather jackets, little James Deans. He and Carol couldn't keep her in at night; if they gave her a curfew, she ignored it. If they locked her in her bedroom, she crawled out the window when Mitchell and Carol were asleep. Carol confessed to Mitchell that much of her makeup was missing. The liquor in the house was also disappearing, Mitchell knew. She'll settle down, Carol said, but she wouldn't meet Mitchell's eyes when she said it.

On Easter Sunday everyone was busy cooking or setting up for the egg hunt on the town hall lawn. Carol was expecting eight for dinner after church: the three of them plus Mitchell's sister, Evelyn Dunn, her husband, an aunt and two sisters. Easter dinner was Carol's big show. At Christmas and Thanksgiving they all went to the Dunn's, but Easter belonged to her. It was the day she proved to the bloodline Epps that she belonged in this family. She polished her silver and set out the French china from Mitchell's grandmother. She forced forsythia to decorate the table, rolled the linen napkins into silver rings, and dared Evelyn Dunn to find fault with anything. But when she turned on the stove to bake her ham, the gas flame sputtered and died. Carol went outside and banged their propane tank with a slotted spoon. It made a hollow, metallic sound. Empty. Dammit, she swore. Sharon! she yelled, trying to calm her panic. Go down to St. Andrews and tell your father we need more propane or there won't be anything to eat. Now!

Sharon, sleepy and disheveled, bumped down the stairs, rolled her eyes, pulled on a sweatshirt, and rode her bike to the church, which sat next to a tiny graveyard on the main road out of Kinder Falls. Mitchell had been there alone since early morning, as he'd promised to bring the theater's folding chairs upstairs for the overflow crowd that was expected for Easter services.

The smell assaulted Sharon the second she entered the church: cloying, headache-y lilies. She went down the back steps to the empty basement theater. Creepy, she thought. Dim light leaked from the back corner. She didn't call out; she was curious. She snuck closer until she saw her father, seated in front of a makeup mirror dressed only in his undershirt and shorts. She was struck by the paleness of his chest, the slightness of his shoulders. She watched him dip a cloth in water and stroke each of his eyelids, removing a deep blue eye shadow. He dabbed water on his brows, rinsed foundation from his forehead. Then, delicately, he lifted a corner of one false eyelash and worked it slowly away from the lid, then the other. He placed them in a small case. He turned away from the mirror and pulled on his dungarees, buttoned up his shirt, and sluffed on his barn coat.

Sharon backed up into the shadows.

In summer, the town moved its activities outdoors and focused them on children and plants. Sharon turned sixteen and got a job working the night shift at Betty's Diner, 5 p.m. to midnight. Betty's paid Sharon enough money to buy cigarettes and gave her an excuse to stay in bed well past noon, which meant she didn't have to have breakfast, lunch, or dinner with her parents.

It was that summer, the summer Sharon turned sixteen, that Carol allowed herself a few glasses of wine in the afternoon.

She'd given it up years before when Sharon was small, but she found joy in tippling now. She felt affection for things that normally irritated her: the sound of crows or a neighbor's tractor chugging past their house. By the time Mitchell came home from the farm's office in the back barn, she'd be napping; he could get his own supper.

It was also in that summer that Mitchell Epps first heard about the Chevalier D'Eon.

It's in the Catskills, but, as the actor they'd brought in to play Mortimer in *Arsenic and Old Lace* had told Mitchell, it's a whole different world. Bungalows to stay in, an old barn they use for drag shows. You can breathe there, he whispered. He gave Mitchell a little squeeze on the arm. You'll love it. Mitchell blushed all the way down his neck and hurried away from the actor. The man ran after him and caught him by the elbow. I'm so sorry, he said. I didn't mean anything by what I said. It was wrong of me to assume. Please forget it.

But Mitchell couldn't forget. The actor had touched a live wire to Mitchell's brain and they both knew it. He felt he'd been given a loaded shotgun and told to carry it for the rest of his life. One sunny morning in July, he pulled back the safety and cocked the trigger.

Mitchell told Carol he was going to fish the Schoharie River and would be back in two days. He put a tackle box in his Dodge Wagon and drove two hundred miles to Jewett, in the Catskills. Lazy foothills went past his window, grew taller, then retreated to make way for little towns: Oneonta, Harpersfield, Prattsville. The road followed a small creek, wound around a lake, cow fields, alfalfa, and came to a group of shabby cabins in an overgrown field. On the side of a barn were painted the words "Bungalows" and "Entertainment." Several women sipped from martini glasses on the wide front porch of a house. He stopped the car and rolled down his window.

One of the women got up and came toward the truck. You lost, honey?

Mitchell startled at the voice. Male. Short black wig parted on the side, white gloves, a slim black dress, black heels, pearl necklace and earrings. Mitchell had imagined this, but he hadn't imagined what he'd feel. The figures on the porch smiled at him. Cat-eye glasses, fake bosoms, broad shoulders, painted fingernails, cigarettes pressed between red lips. An explosion of deep laughter came from within the house.

I said, you lost, honey?

Mitchell couldn't speak. There were too many voices inside him, too many thoughts. His cheeks were bright red; he could feel it. On the lawn to the side of the house, a man in an emerald-green skirt ran a mower over the grass. The white-gloved vision in the black dress leaned into Mitchell's window. He could smell perfume—something sweet with oranges.

I'm so sorry, Mitchell stuttered. I have the wrong address.

It's okay, sweetheart.

Mitchell bent to roll up the window. A gloved hand touched his shoulder. You sure? Mitchell jerked instinctively, and the man withdrew his hand but held Mitchell's gaze, smiling. Mitchell couldn't look away from the pearls, the lashes, the wig, the bemusement he saw in the eyes. At last, his fingers found the truck's ignition key and he eased out the clutch, pushed the stick into first and gently pressed on the gas. Mitchell moved slowly down the road, glancing back at the brunette in his rearview mirror until she was gone.

He allowed himself to luxuriate in the moment he shared with the stranger in pearls and his heart raced with the thrill of what he'd done. Because what Mitchell wanted, what he'd always wanted, was what he'd seen on that porch. Something that lit him up from the inside, something warm and bright that he could bend toward.

It took all of the five-hour trip back to Kinder Falls for Mitchell to re-inhabit himself. There was so much to hide that his bowels twisted just thinking about it. As he got closer to Kinder Falls, he felt the familiar red rush of shame rise in his face. What was he up to? Mitchell was a man in a world in which men made the wheels turn. He had to do his part. Whatever joy he could find would only be temporary. Like with a hurt bird, he thought. You tape up the wing, feed it, keep the bird warm. The bird heals and is happy in his new home, crazy with song. But the bird must go back to where it was and be a bird, despite how much it doesn't want to.

When he pulled into his driveway, Mitchell was fully back to being the man who needed to get someone out to fix the baler. He felt embarrassed for the men on the porch of the Chevalier. What if their bosses could see them like that.

You're back early, Carol said. She stayed huddled in her corner of the couch, didn't get up to greet him. Her skin looked pale and the dark smudges under her eyes seemed deeper than Mitchell remembered. Her hands kept fluttering up to her hair, then flopping down into her lap, over and over. Her eyes looked past him.

Sharon's pregnant.

Mitchell put down his suitcase. His legs felt heavy.

Did you hear me? She's pregnant.

He looked toward the stairs. How?

Honestly, Mitchell?

You know I don't mean how. I mean who?

She won't say. She won't talk to me.

Should I try?

Carol looked up to the ceiling and moaned. Then she lay her head on the coffee table. Do you really have to ask?

Okay, okay, Carol. I'll talk to her.

He climbed the stairs and knocked on the door to Sharon's

bedroom. Opened it. His daughter was leaning against her headboard, legs stretched long on the bed. She was too tall for it. Her feet were dirty with a white stripe where her sandal strap had been. Her sweatshirt hung off one shoulder.

I'm keeping it.

Who's the father?

Sharon shrugged.

They'll make you leave school.

So?

And leave all your friends.

I don't have any friends.

Honey, you're barely sixteen.

Old enough to know what I want. Old enough to say so.

Your mother and I are worried—

Yeah, yeah. You're only worried about what people will think. Your reputation. She gave Mitchell a sly grin. Does mom know? I bet mom doesn't know.

Know what?

What you do at the theater.

Mitchell swallowed. Inside his head, a sudden, cold rain. What do I do at the theater?

I saw you. On Easter. In makeup. Are you a pervert or something?

Mitchell took a step toward Sharon, blood rushing to his face, his fists.

What's going on in here, Carol said, filling the doorframe.

Nothing, Sharon said. I'm keeping the baby. Daddy thinks it's a good idea.

Over my dead body, Carol said. Mitchell, tell her. We'll put the baby up for adoption. It's the only way.

Mitchell took Carol's arm and led her out of the room and downstairs. Let's give her some time, he said, his voice weak.

Carol, defeated, went back to the couch.

They listened to Sharon slamming around in her room. Pregnant as a teen! Carol muttered, shaking her head. She felt the shame of it as if it were a fourth person in their house.

Months passed. Sharon grew plumper and boys stopped coming around. By December, the entire town knew that Sharon Epps, daughter of the biggest landowner in Kinder Falls, great-great-great-granddaughter of the town's founder, spoiled, mean, bratty Sharon Epps was in trouble. But Sharon wore her belly like a weapon, intimidating teachers and classmates as if daring anyone to judge her. Carol took to spending days on the couch, soap operas blaring.

It's not going to be easy, you know, Mitchell told his daughter, as he and Sharon watched snow fall on the fields. It was morning, the kindest time in their house, and Mitchell had made cocoa. He gave her a mug. I mean raising a kid. Distracting them from things they're not supposed to touch. Making them sleep when they don't want to. Fooling them into eating food they say they don't like. The more they grow, the more they push, the more you fight. You wore us out, Sharon. That's why this happened to us.

Sharon's mouth twisted into something ugly. This happened to us? This is about me, Dad, not you. Not Mom. Me.

A solitary red fox leapt through the drifts. In the hen house, the chickens clucked their alarm.

Second Sunday of March, two weeks before Easter, and Mitchell told Sharon they were going to pick up a hi-fi player from the RCA outlet factory north of Kinder Falls. It was a pretty day for a drive, and Sharon was uncharacteristically chipper; it seemed to Mitchell that the more pregnant she was, the better the three of them got along.

Once they left Kinder Falls, she shifted her massive body on the car seat and looked straight at him. I don't really think you're a pervert, Dad. Sharon's voice was light. What you do, you know. Wearing makeup like a girl.

Mitchell concentrated on the road. His mind worked furiously. He could invent an explanation for what she'd seen, something about the theater, something he'd been asked to do, but he knew she'd hear the lie.

What you saw in the theater, it was make-believe, like being in a play, he said. I wanted to be, I don't know, maybe someone else for a few moments. To see what it was like. To be different, I guess.

Do you wish you were a woman?

No, that's not it. I think being a woman is harder than being a man, as far as what people expect of you.

You can say that again.

I can't explain it, Mitchell continued. I looked so different. It made me happy.

You don't want to be who you are?

No, I want to be more of who I am.

Sharon rolled her eyes. So, you're a homosexual?

No, no. That's not it. I don't want to be with men. I love your mother. What you saw, what I did, it's not sexual.

Sharon unwrapped a Tootsie Pop and stuck it in her mouth. Yeah. Mine wasn't sexual either.

Mitchell glanced over at his daughter, her belly nearly touching the dashboard of the car. What do you mean?

Sharon sucked the pop. You know, how I got pregnant. It wasn't really sexual. I let guys do it to get it over with so we could party.

Mitchell felt the blood rise in his neck, his jaw. He gripped the wheel to still his hands. Guys?

She laughed. God Dad, relax. Not at the same time. It wasn't a big deal. Don't get all weird about it. They were stupid guys. A stupid summer. You know how guys are.

Mitchell tried to keep his voice casual.

So, you really don't know who the father is?

No one from here, that's for sure. But so what? It's my baby now. I've always wanted to have a kid. You know, someone who was all mine.

Sharon stared out the window and clicked the Tootsie Pop against her teeth. Mitchell glanced over at her profile. Her cheeks were as plump now as they'd been as a toddler, and he felt his heart break. There was his little Sharon, riding away from him on her first two-wheeler. His teenage Sharon, disappearing with strangers, a stranger.

His eyes were tearing up so he concentrated on the road. Sharon, sweetheart, Mitchell managed to say, kids don't belong to their parents.

Sure they do. Sharon was kicking her leg happily against the dash. Hey, Dad, what is this place?

They pulled up a circular drive and Mitchell took a suitcase out of the trunk.

Really, Dad. Where are we?

Pit stop. I have business here.

He took her elbow, and they walked up the steps and into an office. A nun with a blueish face sat behind the desk. She looked up and smiled. Hello, Sharon, she said.

Mitchell placed the suitcase on a bench, took his daughter's head in both hands and kissed her on the top of the head. This is what your mother and I think is best for you. This is a good hospital; they'll take care of you. When it's born, your baby will be adopted. Your baby will have a home with two parents.

Your baby will have a wonderful life, and you will too. He held her for a second more.

Sharon, stunned, allowed herself to be hugged. Mitchell thanked the nun and turned toward the door.

Where are you going, Dad? You can't leave. Dad!

He mouthed "love you" and opened the door. Sharon ran after him and held tight to his jacket. The nun went to Sharon, and with a very strong grip, pulled Sharon from her father.

Daddy, no, please, I'll do anything you want, I promise. Don't leave me here! Don't let them give away my baby. Please! Daddy, no!

We'll take good care of her, Mr. Epps, the nun said. She shut the door.

Outside the hospital it was cold. Mitchell's lungs hurt with every breath he drew in. He forced his legs forward to walk, keep walking. He reached into his coat pocket for his car keys. Don't panic, he thought, breathe slower. He slid into the driver's seat and turned the key in the ignition.

The sound startled them—three teenage boys walking across the vacant gray of the parking lot. They were play fighting, gently jostling each other. One unzipped his leather jacket, took something from his pocket. A flask. The smallest one shivered, jumped from foot to foot, rubbed his hands, cigarette between his teeth. Suddenly, the big one jumped up on the hood of Mitchell's car and stared at him for a long moment. Then he slammed his palm against the windshield and spat. Mitchell honked the horn, hard. The kid rolled off the hood of his car, laughing, gave him the finger, and ran to catch up with his friends. Within seconds, they were gone.

Mitchell felt a short, sharp twitch in his hands. They balled into fists, and he smashed them against the dashboard until tiny pricks of blood rose on his knuckles. He hit harder, over and over until, exhausted from the day, from everything, he lay his head on the back of the seat and closed his eyes. When he opened them, the hospital windows glinted in the sun like tiny yellow teeth. He walked back into the hospital, found Sharon sobbing on a hard, wooden bench, picked up her suitcase, took her by the hand and led her out of the building. Sorry, he said to the nun who came after them. We've had a change of heart. Sharon's eyes were wide.

The baby was born April 3 in the Bates County hospital, a girl, tiny, only 5.5 pounds. Sharon named the child Caroline, after her mother, in a moment of teenage flippancy.

She wasn't an easy baby, being so small. The first months were filled with tears and sleepless nights for all of them, which led to flared tempers and mean accusations, slammed doors, and eventually contrite silences. A child who has a child, Carol told Mitchell, does not necessarily become an adult.

Carol refused to be seen with the baby in town for the embarrassment of it. Mitchell, on the other hand, strolled Caroline past shops and playgrounds; he openly adored her. Nights when Sharon and Carol, exhausted, retreated to their rooms, he'd watch the baby in her crib and marvel at the blue movement behind her eyes, and at her mouth, a delicate, wormy thing. He saw Sharon in her and he felt that this was a miracle, a second chance. Caroline was his Chevalier, his joy, the light he could bend toward.

Kinder Falls turned 150 in October of 1959, and the town's celebratory parade was going to be the biggest ever. Mitchell filled his wagon with hay bales, hitched it to his pickup, and drove it to the Grange, where the Mother's Club ladies volunteered to decorate it with flowers made of colored tissues. All the young kids in town had been invited to sit on the bales of hay. His wagon would follow Kinder Falls' oldest residents, who rode in a flatbed truck with a sign boasting "Historic Kinder Falls." He'd painted a sign for his wagon that said, "The Future of Kinder Falls."

Mitchell did all of this for Caroline. He thought she would love to ride on Sharon's lap through the middle of town and see all the people watching and cheering from the sidewalks.

The parade floats waited in the Sears parking lot. And to Mitchell's pleasure, plenty of children showed up and climbed in his wagon. There were those two scamps from the green houses on the point—Carol called them Thing 1 and Thing 2—trying to shove hay down each other's backs, their mothers holding tight to them by the belt loops on their dungarees. There was Lucy Staunch and the little niece that came summers, Marlena, dark-eyed and raven-haired, already a beauty. But no Sharon and Caroline. Mitchell watched for them until the Historic Kinder Falls flatbed rolled out and a parade volunteer waved at him to move forward.

Move it, Epps, shouted the man.

Waiting on a few more, Mitchell shouted back. A gap widened between Historic Kinder Falls and Mitchell's wagon.

You okay, Mitchell? A large woman with a clipboard was standing at his window. Dorie Fish.

Yeah, I'm good. Here I go. He pressed the gas pedal and eased the truck onto Water Street. The crowd applauded wildly as his wagon full of children passed by. Mitchell drove slowly, his eyes fixed on the float ahead of him, on the withered old bodies swaying in their seats, their fleshless arms lifting to wave to the crowd. If he lost focus for a second, he knew, he'd drive the flatbed straight through the damn crowd. He pulled his hat down low over his eyes and gripped the wheel.

Later, Carol told him that Sharon thought the whole thing

was stupid. She'd left Caroline at home with her and gone to the lake with the guy who managed the new pizza shop; he had a boat.

It's okay, Mitchell, Carol said. That baby doesn't know from donuts that she's missed anything.

Mitchell went to Caroline's room. She was sitting up in her crib staring out the window at a group of noisy crows perched high in the elm beside their house. Mitchell looked up at the crows; so many of them. Made the top of the tree shake with their jockeying.

He picked up the toddler and carried her to his truck, still decorated with tissue flowers, put Caroline on his lap, started the engine and pulled onto the road. When he reached Water Street he slowed down and waved at everyone he saw, telling Caroline about the parade, about next year, and how she could wear a crown and a party dress and how all the people would cheer when she went by, the most beautiful girl in town, and the luckiest, because she could be anything she wanted, no matter what anyone said, because that was the most important thing in the world, to be who you are, and he'd always be there to help her, no matter what it took, even if it took her away from him. Tears streamed down Mitchell's face as he talked, as he felt her sweet head relax and lie heavy on his neck. She was asleep, but Mitchell kept talking and talking.

Prescribed Burns

Fire. That's all you need to understand farming. Take what's good, burn what's not, and start over clean. Mitchell did it every year: set fire to his hay fields to kill weevils and weeds. He walked out into the burnt stalks checking for hot spots. The stubble crunched beneath his feet and his boots were black with soot; nothing but char as far as he could see, apocalyptic. Seemed a fitting end. Next year he'd be paid to not plant.

Mitchell's brother Donny was back from Florida and according to Donny, there were thousands, even millions of dollars in the black shale that lay below the Epps farm. Donny explained how within a few years there could be a drill pad and water source pond, access roads and rigs brought up on trucks from Texas. Unlocking the rock, he called it. An outfit in West Virginia would bankroll it. Donny would get a cut as broker, he and his brother would share the mineral rights, and the company would lease the land. All Mitchell had to do was stop farming where they wanted to drill. It was an easy decision.

Money from rocks, Mitchell thought. Only Donny would think of that.

Natural gas drilling is where you want to be, Donny said. They pulled a million-and-a-half dollars out of the shale last year, and those numbers will only go up. The first well would go online in 1965, Donny said; if it was lucrative, they'd add more. Cement mixers, tank trucks, bore holes, diesel engines, rigs, nitroglycerin, hydraulics. Once they hit pay, and he knew they would, these guys would build a pipeline and lease even more land. Donny was over fifty now but he was still as ambitious as a kid. Donny, who had no wife, no children, no grandchild like Caroline, who was reading at a fifth-grade level and her, barely six.

Mitchell knew well that the next thing was always coming. What Mitchell didn't know was that Donny would have someone torch the abandoned houses that squatters lived in so he could build his access roads through them. He didn't know that of the eleven sites the Mineral Resources Corporation of West Virginia promised, only two materialized, and those two wells quickly blew through to salt water. Neither brother could know that the Mineral Resources Corporation of West Virginia would give up on the Epps land, cart away the machinery and move on to Ohio, leaving unplugged orphan wells, contaminated water, and bald patches of dirt—dust in the heat, mud in the rain, flat frozen skids in winter.

In the end, Mitchell Epps played his part in the waning of the Epps dynasty by doing nothing in the face of his brother's enthusiasm. He wasn't the cause; he simply let the future unspool in the path of least resistance. In his later years, like the unmaintained access roads Donny had built, Mitchell himself would become rutted, narrow, and harder to negotiate.

Sure, he told Donny. Take what you need.

Avon Calling

1965

Carol

Carol Epps stood on the Morris's porch listening to the chat of the seven women waiting inside.

Ed Sullivan Sunday night   scuff marks on the piano bench   skipped a grade   can't really buy anything   rummage sale at St. Andrews   left the gizzards in the bird   got torched I heard   white go-go-boots dancing in a cage   dark so early   church basement's too cold for Bible study   paid him not to grow corn   roads won't last long   can't find enough sopranos   and the noise!   too smart for her own good

Ding-dong, Carol said under her breath. She put on her Avon Lady smile, opened the door, and strode into the Sheila Morris's living room.

Carol was good at selling Avon beauty products because she wasn't a kitten-heeled department store clerk who didn't know these women; she was simply Carol, married to the handsome farmer, Mitchell, mother to—what would they say?—*go-go boots dancer Sharon,* grandmother to the *too smart for her own good* Caroline. Carol, who lived in the farmhouse above the lake with a fifteen-foot-tall tower and drill out her bedroom window and a constant rumble of trucks that shook her dear, dead mother's fragile teacups in the china cabinet.

Carol placed her Avon sample case on Sheila Morris's coffee table and opened it reverently. This, she began, lifting a golden tube and rotating the barrel so the coral-colored missile rose up, is this year's sensation. "Coral Cream Bliss." And this, she said, lifting an elegantly shaped bottle, is the match: "Coral Cream" nail polish. Next, she hoisted a gift package decorated with daisies. And for our little ladies, Carol said, see how adorable? I gave "Daisy Dust" talc and "First Recital" bubble bath to our granddaughter Caroline for her seventh birthday and she simply loved it. I know your granddaughter would love it too, Marion, don't you think?

But when Carol had presented the gift, Sharon had rolled her eyes, and although Carol had explained that "First Recital" was just the name of the talc and she hadn't meant anything by it, she did wish Sharon would let Caroline take the after-school dance classes at Ruth Charles's Dance studio, which is actually a basement in a house across town, but it had a ballet barre and a mirror, and each spring the girls put on a dance show wearing the most beautiful tutus. You can't be stingy with motherhood, Carol told Sharon. Sharon had looked at her and laughed.

Christmas is coming and so are visitors, Carol chirped, passing around the Avon Hostess Sampler with its miniature soaps packaged like bonbons. She trilled the names and tapped a painted fingernail on each little shape: "Topaz," "Cotillion," "Here's My Heart," "Persian Wood," "To a Wild Rose." You bought this last year, Mary Beth. Wasn't it lovely? And for your mother or mother-in-law—here Carol knit her eyebrows in concern—a hormone cream for women who have older, *uncomfortable* skin. She smiled. Our mothers deserve this kind of special care.

Who was she kidding, Carol thought. Mothers were tied up and thrown off a cliff for monsters to eat. They were burned to the ground to make room for new growth, surrendered at every battle. Mothers were sacrificial.

And this one? Janet Kent asked, pointing at one of the shiny golden bullets in Carol's case. Ah, Carol said, our "Pinky-Dink" lipstick! It's new this season. She twirled the tube and expertly drew a creamy smear on the back of Janet's hand. Demure, don't you think?

The lights flickered and the women sat back and waited. Someone made a joke about the town drunk crashing into a light pole. Everyone tittered. Minutes ticked by. Then the room went black. No one moved.

They'll come back on, Sheila Morris said. Wait a minute or two.

Janet pulled back the front drape. It's the whole town, she said.

Even the streetlights?

Everything. It's pitch black out there.

The women sat still, not knowing what to do. Finally, Sheila spoke. I'll get your coats. I'm sure we all want to be with our families until this fixes itself. Right?

The ladies carefully made their way through the dark to their cars. Eleanor Brouwer got to hers first and turned the beams on so the others could find their keys. Carol, Sheila, and Janet—who lived next door—watched the procession leave, a slow line of red taillights heading into the black.

The Morris boy came charging downstairs with the Kent boy, both breathless. What's happening? What's wrong?

Nothing's wrong, Neil, Sheila Morris told her son. The lights will be back in just a few minutes. You watch.

Janet slipped on her coat. For sure, she said. Come on, Mac, let's get home to Daddy.

Janet's hand was resting on the top of her son's head, and Carol was suddenly undone by the tenderness of the gesture, by

Mac Kent's little-man shirt and rolled-up jeans. I should have had a boy, Carol thought. I'd have been a better mother to a boy.

Oh dear! Sheila said. We didn't get to order anything. I'm so sorry, Carol.

Carol smiled. You know where to find me. She hoisted her Avon case into the car and climbed in. Today was a bust, but she knew she could get Sheila to host again, so all was not lost. She tried the radio, but there was only static; reception was always poor this close to the lake. It was a cold night, a bright cold, and a full moon gilded the edges of the landscape. She drove past the dark motel and the empty A&P parking lot and up the hill through browning vineyards, dying goldenrod, pale cornstalks bent sideways by wind. Tuesday, November 9, 1965. Carol wanted to remember the date in case this was a big event. It was November as well when poor Kennedy was shot; she'd gone to church to pray for him, wept, felt dislodged in the heart. Bad things happened on the shoulder of winter, she thought.

The dark mass of Carol's house loomed ahead. She knew it would be empty. Her husband and granddaughter were at the Dunn's house for dinner, and Carol imagined that they'd stay put until whatever was happening was over, as Mitchell was a cautious driver and he'd hate that all the traffic and streetlights were out. Her daughter, she figured, would stay at work, at the Dewdrop.

Carol dug a flashlight out of the drawer under the hallway mirror and shone it over the living room: aqua Naugahyde couch, wingback chairs, low slung coffee table, sideboard, hi-fi. She checked the television and radio, both dead. Phone, no dial tone; power surge must have knocked out the line. She listened for the train that ran along the back of her fields. Silence. This was the first time in months that she couldn't hear trucks or machinery over at the gas well.

She looked out her bay window at the town below. The darkness was lovely. On any other evening she could see the taillights of cars moving at the speed of blood, but tonight the landscape was a bald pate, still and silent, scalped. It was a different kind of dark, a different quiet. She'd heard the ladies whispering as they left the Morris house: talk of Russian attack, of nuclear bombs, of invasion. Carol thought of Hiroshima. Is this what those people experienced before the bomb fell? This silence, this dark? She felt a pang for little Caroline and her short life. This isn't war, she told herself. This will all make sense later on.

Carol poured herself a glass of wine, opened a bag of M&Ms and bit down on the thin shell of chocolate. She thought about the beef in her freezer that might go bad and wondered if that stuff called hummus Evelyn Dunn gave her—goodness, what even was it?—would mold.

A loud knock made her jump. She clicked off her flashlight.

Please, a man's voice called out, is there gas in your car?

Carol tiptoed to the front door and put her ear to the wood.

My car, the man said, it's run out. I only need a gallon to get home. I'm over on the west side of the lake, on Platt's Hill. There was a pause. I'll pay you back.

He sounded like a young man, maybe even a boy. Carol opened the door a crack. A fellow smiled at her, a shy, polite-seeming smile. She shined the flashlight in the stranger's face and he took a step back. He was barely a man, maybe in his early twenties like Sharon; maybe they even knew each other. He seemed harmless.

Carol tilted the flashlight away from his eyes. Didn't mean to blind you, she said. I think I've got a few gallons in my tank. But I don't know how you'd get it out.

I can siphon it, the man said. He pulled a piece of rubber hose out of the pocket of his army jacket. All I need is a bucket.

Whoa, Carol thought. She eyed him carefully. Boy, man, she couldn't decide in the dark. He sounded sincere. And, she reasoned, he could have stolen the gas and she'd have never known, but here he was, asking politely. She nodded. I'll bring a bucket.

Carol's stockings were sheer and the cold bit at her legs. She pointed her flashlight at the car and watched the young man unscrew the gas cap, feed one end of the hose into the tank, and put the other end in his mouth. After a minute he spit, pointed the hose into the bucket and filled it halfway with gas. Then he raised up the hose to stop the flow.

That's all you need? Carol asked.

That'll do it. Thank you, Ma'am. I've got a funnel in my car.

They stood in the driveway staring at each other. Carol's flashlight made a circle on the gravel.

Have you got something I could use to wash my hands? A hose, or pump, maybe?

Carol considered. There was no water anywhere close outside. And if she let him inside, something really bad might happen. But if something bad was going to happen, it probably already would have happened. She couldn't sense any evil in this kid. Thick glasses, hair curling over his ears, eyes too close together, like a monkey. Skinny. Carol felt she could pick him up and throw him if she had to. Besides, if she said no, what would he think of her? That she was heartless? The thought pained her. Sharon had called her heartless just this morning. She'd been furious, shouted at her. Caroline's tiny! She's got a tiny bladder! Lots of kids wet the bed.

Carol had been very careful with her voice; she didn't want a big argument. I only asked that Caroline put her soiled sheets in the hamper. I thought she should take some responsibility, was all she said.

Sharon's face had gone dark. Don't you dare. What she eats, what she wears, when she sleeps, what she's afraid of, you don't get to do that to her. She's mine. Leave her alone!

Carol had stared down at the puddle of sheets as the washer filled with soapy water. A door slammed upstairs. She'd let herself cry briefly, then straightened her spine, took a breath, and emptied the dryer.

She wasn't heartless. The young man was shivering, rubbing his palms together, shoulders hunched against the cold. Come on inside, she said.

Carol pointed the flashlight at her kitchen sink. The man took his time soaping his hands and rinsing them. He cupped them and rinsed out his mouth. He glanced at the wine bottle on the counter. Carol wished she hadn't left it there.

I'd be so grateful, Ma'am, he said, if I could sit for a minute. I don't feel so great. Maybe I swallowed some gas, I don't know. He reached for the kitchen chair and sank down.

Would he try to rob her after all?

A sudden fizz and a loud bang, like a generator shorting out, rolled across the back fields. Russians! Carol thought, panicking. She counted silently to ten but there was no flash of light, no explosion. She lit a utility candle and put it on the kitchen table. Her hand was shaking.

It was as if the young man read her mind. I don't think it's the Russians, he said. They wouldn't bother with us up here in the middle of nowhere. They'd drop the bomb on New York City. Or Washington. I think it's something else. I saw something really strange out there. He grew quiet.

What? Carol asked. What did you see?

There was a big clearing, like a landing strip, the man said, and there was a probe, like from an alien spaceship—

Carol snorted, short and loud. The kid stared at her. Did you see this probe a few hundred feet from here maybe? she asked.

Yeah.

It's not aliens, honey. They're drilling for natural gas out there. Definitely an earthly thing. Trust me. I look at that mess every day. Carol poured herself another wine, then got a second glass and poured one for the boy. Here, she said, this will take that taste out of your mouth. I'm Carol. She extended her hand.

Luke.

Nice to meet you, Luke.

Nice to meet you, Carol. And thanks for letting me sit here a minute. It's a weird night.

Yes, it is. But it's not an invasion from outer space and it's not a nuclear war. And if I'm wrong, we'll all be dead soon and it won't matter. So, you say you live on the west side?

Yeah. Platt's Hill. In the Estes Park.

Ah, Carol thought, a trailer. That made sense. Tell me about yourself, she said. Did you grow up here? Any brothers or sisters? Are you in college? Do you know my daughter, Sharon Epps? She works at the Dewdrop over in Hydesdale.

Hold on, Luke said, slow down. Didn't grow up here, one brother, I'm not in college, didn't ever go, and she sounds familiar, but I couldn't say.

She's about your age. Dark hair, a little heavy.

I don't think so.

Why didn't you go? Carol said. To college?

He smiled at her. I don't need someone else telling me what to think. He nodded toward his empty glass. May I? he asked. Carol was flattered; the young man seemed to be enjoying her company.

She poured him another glass. You live alone?

He gave a short chuckle. I do now. My girlfriend split two weeks ago.

Oh dear, Carol said. Were you together long?

Three months, Luke said.

Ah, Carol said.

Luke shivered and rubbed his ankles with his bony hands. Yeah, well. I was thinking of heading west anyway, making a change.

West to Ohio? Carol asked.

Luke looked at her and grinned. A scar on his cheek wrinkled weirdly in the candlelight. No, San Francisco. In California.

I know where San Francisco is, Luke.

They stared into the dark, sipping their wine. There was too much little boy in this man, Carol thought. Something unhatched.

So, Carol said, making her voice brighter. Do you work?

Sure, Luke said. You?

I sell Avon beauty products. What do you do?

I'm in the trades.

Which one?

I'm a poet.

Blood bloomed on Carol's cheeks. Was he making fun of her? She got up, opened the front door and looked outside. There was a rustling in the bushes. She swept her flashlight over the yard. Eyes, six or seven pairs, huddled together. Raccoons. Animals taking back their kingdom. Carol thought of Mitchell and Caroline at the Dunns, Sharon at the bar. They all seemed so far away. Something soft brushed her ankles and Randall, their cat, hurried into the house. On a normal night she would have made him stay in the barn, but tonight was not normal. She shut the door.

Luke was staring at the empty fireplace. You want me to build a fire? he asked. It's getting pretty cold in here.

The young man did look cold; so skinny he was, and pale. It dawned on Carol that he wasn't in her house because was enjoying her company, it was that he probably wouldn't have any heat back in his trailer. She thought about that for a minute, then decided she didn't care. Sure, she said. A fire would be nice.

Carol gathered a few more candles and placed them around the living room. She sat on her couch and watched him stack logs in a teepee-like shape, then stuff it with newspaper and light it. Nicely done, she said.

Boy Scouts, Luke said. He got the fire going, then sat on the other end of Carol's couch watching the flames catch on the logs and grow. His knee jiggled and Carol wrapped both hands tight around her wine glass to keep from reaching out to make it stop. He was a mess of tics and twitches. Poor kid.

Carol? Luke asked. Do you smoke?

I used to, she said. I loved it. But Mitchell hated that I did. My husband.

Mind if I do?

Of course not.

Luke dug into his jacket pocket held up a small wad of tin foil and a pipe. Not cigarettes, he said. This. He smiled shyly. You want some?

Carol was confused. What is it?

Hash. It helps me relax.

Oh, I don't think so, Carol said. She watched as Luke peeled off the tinfoil, took out a tiny brown lump, placed it in the bowl of his pipe, and used the candle flame to light it. He sucked on the pipe and exhaled a faint stream of smoke.

You sure? he said, offering the pipe to Carol.

On any other night, Carol would not have done this. She

would not have let a stranger into her house and she would not have given him wine and she certainly would not have smoked hash. But on this lightless, otherworldly night she wasn't fully Carol. She was a woman on a roller coaster cresting the first hill. She gripped the arm of her aqua Naugahyde couch and took the pipe.

The smoke was hot and harsh. She let a little of it into her lungs, then released it though her nose; it felt wonderful to be smoking again. They passed the pipe back and forth until Carol held up her hand to stop. Her body had a warm fullness, as if she had to yawn but she couldn't. Her head was floating just above her shoulders and felt huge.

You okay? Luke asked her. His voice came from somewhere else, not his mouth, but it was round and comforting.

She nodded. Why San Francisco? Carol asked.

Luke closed his eyes and lay his head back on the couch. He exhaled. I'd like to be more spiritually empowered. And that's where it's happening.

Carol had no idea what that meant. Her chest was tight, like someone had wrapped bakery string around it twice. Thoughts fell out of her head before she could finish them.

Luke lifted himself off the couch and poked at the fire. He noticed the framed photos on the mantle and picked up Sharon's sixth grade school portrait. Is this your daughter? he said. She looks angry.

Yes, Carol said, and her voice echoed in the back of her head. She usually was.

Why?

Carol sighed. Why? She was born that way, my daughter. She's a dark sky, pounding rain, then a sliver of sun, the tiniest bit, then thunder, big, cracking thunder, then more trouble, worse trouble. She is half-weather, half-daughter. A girl-storm.

Luke put the picture down. A girl-storm. Wow.

Carol watched the colors of her living room swim: the orange plaid wingback chair in candlelight like daylilies in the bright sun, the melted vanilla color of her table lamps. Her fingers felt long and graceful. She drummed them, admiring how they fanned out on the coffee table. She felt beautiful. Why did she leave? Your girlfriend?

She went back to an old boyfriend. Guess it wasn't really over.

Carol sighed loudly. You young people go through each other like water. I've been married to Mitchell for over thirty years.

It's nice to find a soulmate, Luke said.

Soulmate? She giggled. Oh, well maybe at first.

Carol sunk back on the couch and closed her eyes, picturing a young Mitchell. He had been such a gentleman—polite, quiet, even bowed a little when he said goodnight like there was a movie playing in his head. When she sat with him in the evenings, she felt they were talking even though it was quiet between them for long minutes at a time. He was handsome too. That had a lot to do with it. Had there been joy? In bed, at breakfast? There must have been.

Carol sat up and shook her head. I'm talking about real marriage, she said. I'm talking about one foot in front of the other. I'm talking about dishes and laundry, saying the same things to each other, asking the same questions. I'm talking about raising a child, raising a child's child. It's work.

Sounds like too much work, Luke said. I don't believe love should be work.

Oh, sweetheart, Carol said. She focused on Luke's too-close-together eyes. In fish, she suddenly recalled, predators have eyes on the sides of their heads, prey on the front, and too close. It was obvious to her, of course, which Luke was. Carol went to the hallway mirror. In the weak light coming from the candles she couldn't decide if she was predator or prey; could be either. She returned to the couch. Tell me some of your favorite poetry, she said.

Luke brightened. Do you know the *Desiderata?*

Of course, she said.

Really? Luke asked.

Everyone who's been to church knows that. Carol stood up, opened her mouth wide and sang in a very loud voice, "Praise God from whom all blessings flow, praise him all creatures here below, praise him above the heavenly host, praise Father, Son, and Holy Ghost." When she sat back down she was breathless and delighted with herself, and Luke was laughing so hard he was red-faced.

What? Carol asked, her voice a tinkling in the room. What's so funny?

That's the Doxology. Not the *Desiderata.* And he kept laughing, and his laughing was the most joyful sound she'd heard in ages and she joined him, laughing and laughing until she had to stop because she couldn't get a breath in.

What's the *Desiderata?* she asked when she could finally speak.

"Go placidly amid the noise and haste," he began, but a spate of laughing stopped him there.

Carol loved how their voices filled the room like thousands of arcing songbirds. Her heart was beating fast, probably too fast, and she forced herself to take a long breath through her nose.

Why do you sell Avon? Luke asked, when at last he stopped laughing.

I make my own money. It gets me out of the house. And everyone can use a little glamour.

I don't know about that, Luke said. Makeup is so deceptive.

Of course it's deceptive. That's the point of it.

Luke frowned. I never understood why pretty women wear makeup. They're already so beautiful.

Carol smiled at him. Everyone likes to be a bit more.

Luke stared at her for a long moment, then reached out a hand and touched Carol's cheek. Everyone is beautiful as they are, he said.

She held his gaze, trying to quell the confusion in her head, to breathe through the jolt that ran through her body. Did he think she was beautiful or was he teasing her? His touch was kind. But was she desirable, did he want her?

Luke moved closer.

Carol's heart pounded so hard she was sure he could hear it.

Carol? he said, moving closer still. Can I lay down on your lap?

What?

I feel so tired. Can I lay down?

Carol lifted her arms, and Luke lowered his head and closed his eyes. She sat stiffly, not knowing where to put her hands or gaze, afraid to move her legs. She could smell the sweat from his head, a faint mildew from his army jacket. She felt silly—of course he wasn't going to kiss her; she was probably as old as his mother—but more than that, she felt immense relief.

Now what, she thought. Luke's head was warm on her thighs, like the comfortable weight of a cat on her lap, a child, her child, her grandchild. Carol sighed and stroked Luke's forehead.

Where did you get that scar on your cheek? she asked.

Fishhook.

Fishhook?

Dad was teaching me to cast off a boat. I was twelve. I botched the cast and caught the hook with my cheek. I yanked on the line because I didn't know what else to do. Made it worse. Got the thing stuck deeper in my cheek.

How awful, Carol said.

I remember lots of blood. I remember my dad holding a rag to my cheek with one hand and steering the car home with the other and that he wouldn't look at me. I couldn't figure out if he was mad at himself or mad at me, or just scared at what mom would say when she saw me come home with a fishhook in my face. We all went to the ER to have a doc take it out. Twelve stitches.

Carol watched a tiny vessel pulse on Luke's neck. She pictured the fragile network of veins and arteries that kept him together, kept him whole. A child caught on a fishhook. Pain if you reel him in, pain if you cut him loose; either way, there's a permanent scar. On both of you.

She shifted her gaze to the coffee table where the Kennedy children stared back at her from the cover of a *Look* magazine—those poor, beautiful children. Tender-white like the insides of eggshells. She suddenly feared for everything. For the tiny soldier-boy who saluted the President's coffin on that awful day in '63. For this man-child sitting on her couch. For Mitchell and the quiet inside him she'd never know; for Sharon, her spiky-shell girl-storm; for bright, so-blonde-you-could-almost-see-through-her Caroline. Precious. Fragile. Terrifying.

I didn't even know she was in touch with him, Luke said. When did she do that? How? How did I not know? Luke sat up and slapped his forehead. I'm an idiot.

Randall the cat leapt off the highboy and bounded into the kitchen.

Carol concentrated. They were talking about the girlfriend now. Give it time, she said. You can't just pinch off love like a dead bloom.

What? Luke said.

Like a dead bloom, you know. On a flower. Love. You can't unlove.

What is that supposed to mean?

I'm not sure.

Luke slumped back on the couch.

I need some water, Carol said. My stomach feels hot.

She went to the sink and poured herself a glass of water. The moon had shifted in the sky and cast a slanted light across the back field. She looked at her reflection in the window. Her hair was soft and full, like it was hair from another time in life, or another lifetime, where she was a ballet dancer, or an equestrian, or June Lockhart, and she could make out only the vague outline of her face. Then she looked harder.

Luke!

Carol's heart slammed in her chest. Luke jumped up and ran to her. What?

She pointed. People, dozens of people, were picking their way across the field. Some held hands, some were children. All of them, she understood, were heading for her house.

Carol and Luke stood at the kitchen window, unable to move.

The crowd grew closer. Carol grabbed two cast iron pans from their hooks, handed the larger one to Luke. She pulled him to the back door and put a finger to her lips. Carol could hear their talk growing louder: two men were arguing. She heard the swish of slips under skirts, the click of heels on her flagstones. She heard a knock, tentative. Then, a child crying. Pitiful. She couldn't bear it. Carol opened the door a crack.

A man and woman with a baby stood leaning on each other. Please, Mrs., said the man, could you help us? The train, and they gestured back across the field, is stopped; it's been stopped for two hours, the toilet is broken, my wife needs a bathroom, and we'd be so grateful if we could use yours?

Carol was not thinking anymore, she was floating above her body watching herself stand at the doorway, smiling. Of course, floating Carol said, and she opened the door wide until more than a dozen people filed into her home, all of them thanking her and telling her about the train and where they were supposed to be and what the last few hours had been like: no food, no water, no toilets, no light, no heat. She and Luke placed their skillets on the counter and Carol took out a pitcher and filled it with water and looked for something like a lollipop to give to the children; there were three of them, all under five, one, an infant. The baby's mother looked panic-stricken. Carol hugged her and touched the baby's cheek. Don't worry so much, she said. The baby will feel it.

She lit more candles.

The people from the train had different theories about what was happening, but most seemed to believe there was trouble in the world and that this was the beginning of something awful, rather than the sudden end of their lives. A man in a striped suit thought it was nothing to worry about. Some electrical problem somewhere, he said. They'll fix it and everything will be back to normal. One of the children asked if Santa would come at Christmas if there were no lights, and her mother said, yes, of course he would, and then burst into tears. Khrushchev, muttered a heavy-set man with an orange woolen hat. He's sabotaged the whole country, no doubt about it. A dark-haired man clasping a briefcase glared at him. I'm trying to get home to my kids, he said. Can you shut up? Luke lit a cigarette for a blonde in bell-bottoms who was looking out the bay window. I wouldn't mind living without electricity, she sighed. It's beautiful, don't you think? Totally, Luke said. Two young men also lit cigarettes and the living room filled with smoke. An elderly woman with a huge bosom covered her nose with her handkerchief and looked disgusted. A man in blue overalls was talking excitedly about how he saw a fireball in the sky the moment before the lights went out. Castro, muttered another.

No, Khrushchev, said the bald man. Extraterrestrials, said the man in overalls. The government knows more than they tell us. Luke swiped the wine bottle to share with the blonde. Carol cracked a few windows. She could make out a pair of coyotes circling each other near the hedges. One snapped and she heard a sharp whine. The cat! she thought, alarmed. Was Randall still inside? She scanned the living room. The man in overalls and a college kid in a fringe vest were in the kitchen arguing about Kennedy and if he'd really done the right thing with Cuba, and the baby began to cry. There were not enough chairs for everyone to sit, and the very large-bosomed woman asked the man with the orange woolen hat to stand up and let her sit, and the man pretended not to hear her. She sat down dramatically on the floor and the cat, startled, ran out from under the couch, up the drapes, and onto the top of the bookshelf, which started everyone nattering, and Carol had finally had enough.

She slammed her cast iron skillet on the countertop. The room went silent.

I'm making chocolate chip cookies, she announced. She dragged her biggest bowl out from under the counter. You, she said to the weeping woman with the young child, measure me six cups of flour in this. And you two—she pointed to the men arguing about Kennedy—hand me all the milk and butter that's in the fridge. And in the cabinet over your head, there is a bag of chocolate chips.

The people from the train watched transfixed as the ingredients went together—butter, sugar, flour, baking soda, chocolate chips—then got spooned onto baking sheets. Carol lit the propane stove and popped the trays into the oven. The people waited quietly. When the first batch was done, Carol took the cookies out to cool. Without a word, they all lined up. The children were ushered to the front of the line, then the women, then the men. They seemed of one mind: If they were all going to die in an atomic bomb blast, they would die civilized human beings.

It was a failure near Ontario, Canada: a faulty relay switch the size of a pack of cigarettes caused the outage, which began at 5:16 p.m. and cascaded from Niagara through the Northeast, causing the first major power outage in American history. Surgeons in Albany completed their operations by flashlight. People were trapped in elevators, the National Guard directed traffic, strangers held hands, and department store employees rested in display beds. In Kinder Falls, the train conductor got word through a transistor radio, followed his passengers to Carol's house, and gave them the news. At 8:20, the lights flickered on. Everyone cheered and hugged each other. The passengers walked back through the field to their train, now glowing like a string of diamonds. The coyotes, wary, went back to the peace of their rock crevices.

Luke gave Carol a side hug. He looked at her for a long while. How'd you know to do that? To make cookies?

Everybody needs something, Carol said, you just have to figure out what it is. And sometimes everybody needs the same thing.

You're pretty cool, Carol.

Damn straight, she said. In the bright light of her living room, she could see he was older than Sharon, maybe in his thirties, too old to be a poet. Carol stood in her doorway and watched Luke head to his car with her bucket of gas and the blonde; he was giving her a ride home. The blonde held tight to the bag of Avon samples Carol had given her.

Desiderata. She'd look it up.

She picked up the last few cookies and sat down to eat them. They were still warm, and they filled her mouth with melted chocolate so much sweeter than any M&M. She glanced over at the photo of Sharon on the mantle. She was just a little girl then, Carol thought, with only little-girl powers. Vulnerable like a hatchling, hungry to be fed. And Carol had tried to feed her, and she was still trying, and could only do that in the ways she knew how, and she was still learning how, and getting better at it, or at least she thought she might be. She understood that she was the mother, would always be the mother, sacrificed and essential both at once, and when Mitchell, Caroline, and Sharon came home at last, she felt the stirrings of old love in her heart.

3

THE CHILDREN OF
KINDER FALLS

The children of Kinder Falls are not allowed to watch television in the summer. They are expected to be outside searching for fossils in dry creek beds or scouring weeds on the side of the road for soda bottles they could turn in for cash. But early on June 6 in the summer of 1966, mothers called their children indoors, sat them on the floor in front of the television set and told them that something amazing was going to happen. The children were annoyed at being called in to watch news. Shush, the mothers said. Astronauts are coming. Astronauts! Astronauts were like God—you never saw them but you knew they were up in the sky somewhere, floating among the stars in outer space. Outer space! For endless minutes the children watched staticky fog and ocean waves play across the screen. They grew bored and complained. One of the mothers, Sheila Morris, hushed everyone with an upraised finger and pointed at the screen. The women leaned in. One held a tissue to her lips, closed her eyes, and silently mouthed a prayer.

Faintly, through fog, a crane lifted a salt-shaker shape onto a boat. That's it? one of the boys asked. That's the spaceship? The door of the capsule opened. A bald head popped out. The mothers laughed with relief. It's a miracle, Sheila Morris said, all the way to the stars and back! You won't often see something like, kids!

The children were confused. The astronaut looked like

their fathers, with his bald head and stern face. A normal man, who could live in Kinder Falls. They could have seen him at the gas station. But the mothers beamed at their children, their hearts full. On this day, at this moment, it was possible that one of their little boys—all scrapes and freckles now but not forever—would grow up to become an astronaut, would walk on the moon, would have their names in a history book. Such a brilliant, happy, promising day it was.

The Edge

1966

Mac & Neil

If you go swimming in the lake
Don't go alone for goodness sake
Mavis Staunch is down below
She'll catch and drown you by the toe

August, and the grapes were still green, hard, and sour.

Stop singing that stupid song, Neil said. He and Mac were lying on their bellies, binoculars trained on the dock a football field away.

What song? Mac said. This song? *If you go swimming in the lake—*

Neil and Mac were both eleven and skinny, but all the boys on Okisee that summer were skinny. Neil was a Morris, pale and blonde like his mother, hairs barely visible on matchstick calves, bangs grown long like Ilya Kuryakin in *The Man from U.N.C.L.E.* His voice squeezed through his nose, always would. Mac Kent was built like fatwood: short and dense. He was a good son in the way you could be a good son in 1966. He put away dishes, took out the garbage and burned the paper trash, shoveled the driveway in winter, and fed the dog twice a day. He also did the things no one knew about: washed dried blood from his father's pillowcase, emptied the pee bucket, and checked the gauge on his oxygen tank. Those things Mac hated.

The sound of a splash cut through the haze of dawn. Neil jumped. See, I told you!

It was a fish, Mac said.

Wasn't a fish, Neil insisted.

The mid-sixties brought a group of hippies from New York City to work the Ukrainian's vineyards on the west side of the lake. They were all living in the Tuttle's stone house, and Neil had heard that they swam nude early in the morning at Harold's Point.

Neil cocked his head. Look. The dock over there.

The boys sat up and raised their binoculars.

On the other side of the little cove, a girl looked up at the sky and hugged herself.

It's only a summer kid, Mac said, letting his binoculars hang on his chest. And she's not naked.

A loud rumble drifted over the lake with a gust of wind.

Goddam Epps drilling, Mac said.

Goddam Epps, Neil said, and spit.

A light went on in the pale green house nearest them. Neil's.

Your mom's up, Mac said.

That's weird. She's not usually up this early on a Saturday.

Neil! Mrs. Morris called out from the back door. Something was wrong. Her voice sounded tight, like drumskin.

Neil left Mac and hurried inside.

When Neil came back to the dock his face was pale and his words came out in short bursts as if he didn't have enough air to string a sentence. My mom said. She said. She heard. That kid from South Carolina.

They could both picture it. The waterfall at the end of the Schuyler's creek was forty feet straight up. Wasn't much of a falls, mostly a trickle that fell into a shallow pool that was always cold. You get to the top of the falls by cutting through the vineyards that sloped up from the two-lane.

They all did it: pretended to jump, pretended to push each other. But they knew that no one could trust flip-flops, especially at the end of the summer when the rubber bottoms were worn smooth. They knew the distance between their bodies and the edge. Between them and the thing you couldn't take back. The kid didn't know because he wasn't from Kinder Falls, and he was probably a clown. Dead because he was a clown.

Mac shook his head, trying to take it in. That kid was down at Reed's Drug yesterday. I saw him buy fireballs.

The boys paused to imagine what a kid would look like who'd fallen forty feet onto rocks, but there were no images they could fix on. The only death they knew were squirrels, deer, fish.

Mac's mother stepped out onto her porch.

Gotta go, Mac said.

Neil got out his bike and rode to St. Andrews church. He slipped in the side door and stretched out on the last pew underneath the crucified Jesus attached to the wall. The church was dark and Neil could hear his own breath. He closed his eyes against the tears. A bicycle parked by the boat launch could have belonged to the kid. Footprints dried in the mud, a sneaker stranded by the side of the road, a popsicle stick floating in a puddle, they all could have been the dead kid's. Dead. Neil felt the punch of the word in his body. He reached up to touch the cold, polished foot of Jesus but couldn't find any comfort. The summer was ruined.

He pedaled to Schuyler's creek, dropped his bike in a tangle of wild carrot, and climbed through the vineyards to the top of the falls. He stepped carefully on the smooth, algae-covered rocks until he was close enough to look over at the shallow pool below. He wanted to see. He wanted to imagine how it happened, what it might have felt like. Maybe flying, at first, and maybe you think an angel will catch you, or maybe you black out so you don't feel any pain when your body hits the rocks. Neil inched closer to the edge of the falls, looking for footprints in the green muck. Because they wouldn't be there. Because kids didn't die.

Hey, a voice said, and Neil backed up from the edge. He felt a warmth at his back. When he turned around, he thought he saw the kid standing there, with one hand wrapped around a hanging tree branch. Cutoffs, frayed at the hem. Surfer shirt he always wore. Tan legs, tan arms, burned nose. Then he was gone. At first Neil thought it was probably some idiot from his school pulling a prank on him. He squinted up the creek, studied the rocks. Then, he was there again, the kid.

Hey, Neil said.

The kid came up next to Neil and crouched, picked up a small stone, and pitched it over the falls. The rock made a satisfying plop in the pool below. He was fading in and out, like when the sun goes behind the clouds. Neil scraped up a pile of stones and placed it between them. They took turns pitching the rocks and waiting for the sound. When it came, if it hit the deepest part of the pool, it was as good as when a bat meets a slow pitch. When they ran out, they got up to look for bigger ones. The kid pried a flat, home-plate sized stone from the mud. The boys grinned at each other. The kid crept closer to the edge and hoisted it over.

Neil waited, breathless. A few seconds went by. A mosquito landed on his arm and he brushed his face against it. He didn't want to slap for fear any noise would ruin what he was waiting for: the round, resonant, bass-tone smack of flat stone on water. He waited another few seconds, ears straining, hair standing up on his arms. Still no sound. He glanced over at the kid but the kid was gone. Neil had one of those weird feelings, like he wasn't sure what was real. It passed. He was alone. No, he was more alone.

Mac lay on his bed, air drumming to "House of the Rising Sun," hitting the bass drum with his right foot, snare with both sticks. Today, his fantasy bored him. He took out his Brode uniform and ran a finger along the crease in the pants. The school seal was embroidered in gold on the breast pocket. Every time he looked at the uniform, he felt Kinder Falls fade. Even the name—Brode—felt important. The school was eighty miles away to the north. It could already be fall there and cooler, greener, not the dusty yellow that covered acres of hay and wheat around Kinder Falls. When his parents said he would have to repeat the sixth grade, and not in Kinder Falls but at a military school, Mac was relieved. In this uniform he wouldn't be a boy who knew field corn and car dealerships and where to dig for nightcrawlers. He would be the new kid, a stranger. Nobody would know anything about him: his failing grades, his asthma, his fear of snakes.

He told Neil nothing about Brode. He would, at the right time.

Mac, his father called. You forgot—Mac's dad spoke only in half-sentences punctuated by coughing fits—the trash.

Yes, sir, Mac called. Then, under his breath: Sir Hack-a-Lot. At boarding school there were no fathers with late-stage emphysema.

New kids came in the summer like fleas. They were renters: their dads happy for a place on Okisee so close to the racetrack, their moms happy to sit in the sun and cook on a different set of dishes. Mac and Neil never played with the summer kids. There was no point; they would leave after a week or two. But there was something about the dark-haired girl that intrigued them.

The day after they heard about the dead kid, she was standing outside Reed's Drug unwrapping a Turkish Taffy. She wore her Madras shirt unbuttoned, and underneath, a tiny tank top and no bra. A teenage puff of baby fat rolled over her belted denim shorts. She had drawn a swoop of black eyeliner past the outside creases of her eyes like Cleopatra. She looked right past the boys and headed up the street. Her blue-black hair swished with each step she took. Swish, swish, past the post office into Lydell's Fabric Store.

Mac sucked the last of his freeze pop from the plastic sleeve and flicked it onto the street. You think she's someone famous?

Nope. She's the one that comes for a few weeks to stay with her Aunt Lucy.

Who told you that?

Ma. She's friends with Lucy.

She looks like she could be a movie star.

She's only fourteen.

Swish, swish. The girl came out of Lydell's and walked back toward them.

Hey, she said.

Hey, both boys answered at the same time.

She smirked. You know who sells morning glory seeds around here?

Hardware store, Neil said, without knowing.

Cool.

Swish, swish. Away from them.

Neil called out after her. Hey! What do you want the seeds for?

Shut up, Mac hissed.

The girl turned and flashed her violet eyes at them. To get high.

She turned around and kept walking.

The boys stared after her, their mouths chewing nothing.

Swish, swish.

She was a twin, Neil's mother told him. One died in the womb. A sister. Got to be the saddest thing ever. His mother grabbed Neil's chin and looked squarely into his eyes. Be nice to Marlena. She's delicate.

Mrs. Morris was watching her son carefully this summer, perplexed by the boy he was becoming. Neil had always been such a fairy child, so pale and delicate, almost translucent when he was a baby. Now he was opaque. She couldn't tell what was going on in his head. She knew other mothers would chastise her for saying it, but she wished he'd stay away from St. Andrews. The last thing she wanted was a priest in the family.

Mac and Neil's houses fronted the lake. They were separated by a low hedge of forsythia that ran from the beach to the storage shed in Mac's back yard. Both houses were the large-porch-small-rooms construction common along the shore of Okisee, both a pale green. The backyards bordered a weedy hill, where a thin creek ran down the middle from the woods above. The boys knew these woods like they knew their own skin. In the spring, it was ripe with the mushroomy smell of mold. In fall, it was dried leaf dust. In winter, the ground lay beneath snow that reached up the sides of tree trunks like turtlenecks. But it was in the summer that the woods were spectacular: moths clustered like lace on tree bark, bees, mice, and snakes animated the low bushes. If you stood on the frog-shaped rock, you could see the lake in one direction and in the other, pterodactyl-headed pumpjacks sucking water at the pit. What made this strip of trees special, though, was the sugar shack. The shack itself—barely a handful of boards—knelt in the midst of stringy raspberry canes. It was grayed the color of beech bark and softened from years of snow melt, mud, and forest mites. The glass jugs, the few that were unbroken, remained as they'd been left: lined up and empty save for dead flies and leaves.

The boys didn't get to the shack until nearly dusk; the biting bugs would be out soon. Neil was fooling around with a magnifying glass and a piece of straw, trying to get a flame going inside the fire pit he and Mac built with stones.

Too slow, Mac said. He stuffed dried grass and leaves underneath a few twigs and lit it with a Bic. The leaf edges took and glowed. He blew on the tiny embers and the fire spread to the grass, then lit the bottom of the kindling. He backed away and bowed.

Clown, Neil said.

Mac took a Milky Way bar out of his pocket, broke it and offered half to Neil. I gotta tell you something, he said. Neil took the candy and stuffed all of it into his mouth.

Shoot, Neil said.

Mac shook his head. It's no big deal, really.

What.

I'm going to Brode.

Neil stopped chewing. Like when? High school?

No, now.

Like next month?

A plane flew loud across the sky.

They're making me. My dad thinks I need discipline.

Neil was silent. He couldn't go to seventh grade alone.

When did they tell you?

I don't remember. Maybe June, I don't know. After school got out.

Neil lay back and looked up into the canopy that was so thick he couldn't see a single bird. His anger flared and his eyes welled. You knew all summer? he asked. But it wasn't a question.

The woods got louder in the quiet around them. Mac stuck a stick into an ant hole and tiny black ants swarmed his feet. He kicked to knock them off. Asshole ants, he said.

Neil swallowed the wad of Milky Way, felt it move down his throat and lodge there.

Asshole ants, he whispered. The kid had disappeared at the top of the falls. Mac would disappear too. The sun dipped lower, and both the temperature and the light dropped; all Neil could see was an outline of Mac. He took a chance. I saw the dead kid, he said quietly.

Mac gave him a quick look. What do you mean you saw him? After he died?

Yes. After he died. I went to the falls. He was up there, Mac. Honest. As real as you and me.

Don't be a jerk.

It happened, I swear.

You're lying. Why would you even say that, Neil? That's so messed up.

Neil colored bright red. I'm not lying.

You are too.

Okay, forget it. Forget I said anything.

Big fat liar!

I said forget it, asshole.

Mac lunged at Neil, pushed him to the ground and straddled his chest. You saw a dead kid walking around? You can't see people after they're dead, Neil. You can never see them again. They're gone. You're a liar, a stupid liar.

Ow. Cut it out, Mac. Neil tried to wriggle out from under him, but Mac pinned Neil's arms to the ground with his knees.

Was it scary, Neil? Did you pee your pants?

Go to hell, Mac!

Mac hocked up a yellow wad and spit onto Neil's face. Pussy, he said. He picked himself off Neil's body.

Neil sprung up, ran at Mac, and kicked as hard as he could at Mac's groin. Mac let out a guttural yell and swore every word he could think of. He struggled to his feet but Neil was too fast. All Mac could see was a plaid smear running through the woods. Mac stomped out the fire, furious. He limped home and shut himself in his room. After dark, Neil's bedroom light made bright squares on the lawn between their houses. Mac pulled down his shade, put his "House of the Rising Sun" 45 on repeat and turned it up loud.

The day after she heard about the boy dying, Marlena found a deer jawbone on the shore. The lake swallowed lots of bones, but this one seemed special. She soaked it in bleach until it whitened. She removed the four tiny teeth of the lower jaw and glued them to a thin piece of rawhide. This she hung round her neck and headed up the hill away from the lake.

It was too hot for living. There was mud in the ruts dried to the color of nothing. Trees gasped; leaves hung on to branches like cicada husks. The sun burned her forehead and her skin felt too tight. Marlena climbed past the blasted fields to the coolness of the woods. She fingered her deer tooth amulet. The tooth was the dead boy like the wafer was Jesus. She walked until she got to a clearing with a stone fire pit and a few gray-ish boards. She sat cross-legged next to the pit and let the ants explore her thighs. She touched the tooth necklace and conjured up the smell of coconut suntan lotion, the feel of the dead boy's thigh brushing against hers on the bench in front of Reed's Drug. Marlena touched the spot with her finger. Was he still there? The boy had been a boy that she met for a day, but now his life was so big in hers, took up so much of hers, he was like a husband from another time. If she swam in Okisee with all the boys in the world, this boy would be the one she swam to. Marlena saw him in her head, saw him falling from the top of the waterfall, and she gave him wings that bowed with air and lifted him away from the stones. She made everything around him soft, like you could fall into it and it would hold you.

Mac woke early. He lay in bed staring at his ceiling. His legs twitched like a jackrabbit's. He always had to move—run, charge off the end of a dock, throw himself down a grassy hill—anything to change where he was. At night, he'd tangle his sheets, kicking and fidgeting until a charley horse got him in the calf and he had to jump out of bed and try not to holler. He'd look out the window at Neil's house, square like a box of night, and it would comfort him. Mac wanted to call Neil and tell him more about Brode but today it felt cruel.

Neil was trying not to think about Mac at all. When his house got too hot and loud with his mother and her friends, Neil snuck out to the church with his *Strange Tales* horror comic. The plaster walls were damp and the stone floor was cool when he lay down on it. Neil stared at the panels of the snaky monster that haunted the sewers of Taiwan sending grown men screaming for their lives. He imagined himself the warrior with the samurai sword slicing the monster to shreds, blue-black blood flooding the streets. Jesus looked down on him, and Neil gave him a thumbs-up.

In the late afternoon a summer storm churned the lake and turned the water brown. The wind chipped the surface into whitecaps. Thunder and lightning came at the same moment and rain lashed windows and flooded creek beds. When it was over, dead perch were tangled in the seaweed along the water's edge. Mac and Neil both had the same impulse: check the sugar shack before it got too dark. See if anything was broken, changed. Mac got there first.

The girl was sitting cross-legged on the frog-shaped rock. She wiped at her face and squinted up at Mac through thick eyelashes.

What are you doing here? he demanded. The clearing was littered with wet leaves and green acorns torn by the storm, but the shack was undamaged.

I found this place yesterday, she said. I like it here. She held up a maple leaf. See this? Everything is connected. The veins in this leaf are the veins in your body. And spirals—snail shells, pinecones, hurricanes, DNA, galaxies—they're all the same pattern.

Mac didn't know where to put his eyes.

What was this place? she asked.

Maple sugar shack, Mac said. Where they boiled it down. He was sweating. Her stare seemed to suck him five feet closer. He pulled his T-shirt up and wiped his face. The girl didn't take her eyes off him. With this girl in it, the woods felt different: there was too much twisty bitterroot, tangles of sumac, poison ivy twining around the trunks of old trees. It was too crowded.

Neil came into the clearing.

Ah, Marlena said. Mutt and Jeff.

Neil and Mac glared at each other.

The girl raised her arms like a priestess. Do you sense him? Who?

Don't be morons. The boy that died, he's still here, she said. She stared evenly at the Mac and Neil. Gone is never completely gone.

Neil met her gaze. White skin, straight-cut black bangs. He could see she'd drawn tiny lower lashes on the skin under her eyes. He thought about her having a twin, about having to live in her mother's stomach with a dead baby. He felt sorry for the girl. Maybe that was what she wanted, to be felt sorry for.

He could still be around, Neil said quietly. In purgatory, or something.

Mac whacked him in the arm.

What's your name? Marlena asked.

Neil. He's Mac.

I'm Marlena. She swept her arms like a ballet dancer. This is sacred ground, Neil.

No, it's not, Mac said.

The setting sun slanted into the clearing and Marlena's profile flamed. They all looked up at the sky, going red to violet. Within a half hour it would be dark. Curfew.

Neil, can you build a fire? Marlena said. I need a fire. She turned her gaze on Mac. And you? Will you help?

Mac looked past her at the ruin of the shack. The girl confused him.

Marlena fingered her deer teeth pendant and smiled. Great!

It took longer because everything was wet. The three of them combed the woods searching for things to burn. They gathered a few branches and pine needles along with pieces of road trash that was halfway dry: paper cups, wrappers, newspaper. By the time they finished, a caul stretched across a huge expanse of dark sky. Curfew had come and gone, and Neil and Mac would both be in trouble. Neil named things in his mind to keep from panicking. Salamander. Log. Sloppy grass. Mac thought about the chores he was supposed to get done and dismissed them. He lit the pile with his Bic. The fire sparked and took.

Marlena dropped cross-legged to the ground. We have to tell him it's okay to go. Sit down and look into the flames until you see him, she ordered. She sat tall and inhaled deeply. He'll come.

Neil and Mac fixed their gaze at the fire.

Minutes passed. Fog spread out on the forest floor, slunk through the trees, dissipated, then gathered again. More time went by; the fire rose up. Neil closed his eyes and pictured the kid pitching stones from the top of the falls. Mac threw handfuls of pine needles into the flames. Mosquitos buzzed in their ears.

Marlena closed her eyes and imagined the boy horsing around on the slick, flat stones. She pictured him taking a little run, sliding from one side of the creek to the other. She tried to smell cherries rotting on their branches, feel the breeze ruffling goldenrod and chicory on the banks. She conjured the moment the kid slipped over the edge, imagined his arms tearing at the air, his legs pumping as if he could outrun the fall. But before he hit the bottom, she scooped him up and placed him on a bed of moss. She watched him lie there, panting, his eyes wide with panic. She put a hand on his chest and waited until his breathing became regular. Took her hand off. He flew up into the trees so fast she saw only the colors of him. Her eyes popped open.

We did it! Did you see him go?

The boys stared at the ground and said nothing. Marlena was quiet for a long time. When they glanced up at her, her face was wet with tears.

There were two of me once, Marlena said in a small voice. I don't know why it was me who lived. I still feel her next to me. She won't go.

Mac and Neil searched each other's eyes. *What do we do?* Marlena's crying grew louder and more violent until her whole body convulsed and she made a weird choking sound, as if she couldn't breathe. Neil stood to help but she kicked at him. Get away from me, she croaked.

Go get her aunt, Mac said. Go, Neil. Fast as you can.

Neil ran through the dark by memory. Tree roots and rocks rose up and vanished behind him. His sneakers flew, barely touching the ground, and his arms flailed at branches in his way. He didn't look down, only forward, as if his eyes could pull him faster. When he hit the hill, he ran all the way to Devon Street, to Marlena's Aunt Lucy's house, where he didn't even knock, he opened the screen door and went in, surprising the aunt, who was bent over the finger of her youngest son picking at a splinter with a blackened needle.

The mad hoot of a loon on the lake echoed through the woods. Mac inched closer to Marlena. Hey, hey, calm down, he said quietly. She flung an arm out to keep him away and drew her legs up into a ball, sobbing. Mac waited, not daring to go closer but too afraid to take his eyes off her. When at long last her agitation lessened, he put a hand on her knee. Marlena, you okay? They stared at each other, Mac trying to breathe calmly, trying to coax Marlena's breath to match his, the way he did for his father, the way he knew. Time slowed. They waited, breathing together, until a flashlight flickered in the distance. Neil and Aunt Lucy, coming up the hill. Marlena skittered away from Mac, closed her hand around her necklace and ran. Hey! Mac yelled. He took off after her.

Marlena concentrated on the feeling of running, of having weight and speed, skipping over roots and rocks and under low branches. The Other was gaining behind her, the second-her, the sister who was always nearby and never there. She ran faster; it ran faster. It was so close behind her Marlena felt the heat of it on her back. She ran until her lungs felt like they would pop and she couldn't run another step. She whipped around and faced the darkness. Enough, Marlena thought. She tipped her head back to expose her neck and opened her arms to the night. Here I am! Come here right now and get me. She closed her eyes and waited, heart banging against her ribs, breath coming in bursts. Come on! she screamed. But nothing came. She opened her eyes. All there was, was her. And the boy, Mac, clambering toward her through the tangle of weeds and prickers. She turned her back on him and ran, jumping over dead logs and letting the raspberry thorns tear at her T-shirt.

Stop! the boy screamed at her, there's a big drop! but Marlena had already stopped at the edge of a pit, amazed at what she saw below: construction trailers, parked trucks, pipes, puddles, and an otherworldly green light that illuminated a long-necked giant.

What is that? she asked.

He came to stand behind her, wary, ready to grab her waist if she moved toward the edge. Pumpjack.

What does it do?

Pulls water out of the ground.

Why?

To make the gas come up easier.

How far does it go down?

Really deep. But first they need to break up the rock. Mac gently took Marlena's arm and guided her backward a step.

But if you break up the rock down there, won't the top fall in?

I don't think it works like that.

Marlena thought the pumpjack looked like a giraffe grazing on a savannah, calm like she imagined giraffes to be, their heads bending low, then lifting high up in the leaves where there were no predators. She sighed. It's beautiful, Marlena said.

She shook off Mac's hand. I wasn't going to jump.

I know.

I wasn't, really. I want to grow up more than anything. I want to get married. I want my own house. I want to be famous. I want everything. Don't you?

I never thought about it, Mac said.

She squinted at him. That, I believe.

Neil came into view with Aunt Lucy, a dog, and two boy cousins. The aunt hugged Marlena and rubbed her back. It's all right now honey, you're all right. The cousins stood back a few feet, wary. The aunt nodded at Neil and Mac. Marlena has big emotions, she said. She'll be fine. She took a gentle hold of Marlena's shoulders and turned her toward home. The cousins followed at a distance. Mac and Neil waited until they were all out of sight. They were quiet for a long while. Then they stomped out the fire with their feet.

So that was weird, Neil said.

Yeah.

What were you two doing at the pit?

Mac threw dirt on the last embers. She wanted to know if the drilling really breaks up the deep rock.

Course it does.

She wanted to know if the ground would crumble.

Neil snorted. It doesn't work like that.

But couldn't it?

They know what they're doing, Neil said. Neil gave Mac a quick cuff on the head. You're such a pussy sometimes, Mac.

Yeah, that's me. I'm a pussy.

They walked in silence back toward their houses. There were lights on at Mac's. His mother would be up waiting; there would be punishment for how late he was. Mac's father, though, would be sleeping the sleep of the drugged. Mac thought about Brode, and how, if he was that far away, his father's death might be smaller, like through the wrong end of binoculars.

Neil's house was dark, but the porch light was on for him. The loon waffled again.

She's laughing at us, Neil said.

Mac snorted. She's laughing at you, maybe. He headed up the walk toward his house.

Hey, Neil called after him. What if the moon isn't a moon but a hole in space that opens up to a parallel world? And they invented a rocket that could get you there.

Mac stopped, didn't turn around. It would take too long, he said. We'd be old.

Then, what if time didn't exist so you could always be the same age?

Who'd want to be the same age forever?

I might.

A dry cough came from Mac's house, escalated, abated.

Well, I wouldn't, Mac said.

The silhouette of Mac's mother appeared in the kitchen doorway. She opened the door for him and Mac climbed the porch steps, kicked off his sneakers, walked into the house and was gone.

The loon hoo-hoo-hoo-ed and the sound skipped across the water, louder than the insects worrying the light on Neil's porch, louder than the banging of the jack sucking rock blood beyond the hill, louder than the thwack of flip-flops against Dorie Fish's heels as she walked by Neil's house. Her fat jiggles like she's full of water balloons, Neil thought, and snickered.

Her Mother's Life

Dorie

Unmerciful, that snicker. And mercifully unaware of it, she was. Dorie Fish walked out onto the old Tuttle dock, kicked off her flip-flops, lowered her bottom onto the wood and swung her legs around, kicking softly at the water. In her hand she held her mother's dentures.

When Mr. Dobbs called to say that her mother had passed, Dorie and Sam drove to Wheeling for the funeral and came home with seven boxes—her mother's life neatly arranged by category. Clothing (goodness no, Dorie thought), some nice plates (yes), a shoebox filled with the postcards and letters Dorie had sent over the years (so boring even Dorie couldn't re-read them), eighteen pairs of nylon stockings (what to do with those?), three fox head stoles with beetle-black eyes (hideous), a large store of sanitary napkins (why?), her mother's charm bracelet, and her dentures. Dorie would forget about the dentures for months, but each time she came across them, she wasn't ready to let them go. Mother, she'd think, smiling.

She cradled the teeth in her hands. The thought of her mother without teeth made Dorie laugh, as Annalee had been a vain woman. Dorie looked down the lake toward the lights that twinkled at the end of the Dunn's expansive double dock and felt aggrieved, as she always did when she thought about Mrs. Dunn and all her money. Born to it. Didn't earn it.

Dorie stood up with effort—she was heavier than ever—cocked her arm and chucked the dentures high in the air over Okisee. *Into the lake, Mom.* She closed her eyes and listened until she heard a soft splash, like the innocuous plop of a gull dropping a mussel shell.

Sounds of the nightly news on television drifted across the water. Dorie breathed in the lake's calm. She walked back past the twin green houses in the cove, where she saw Neil Morris looking up at the sky through binoculars. She watched him for a minute. Dorie was always touched by the sight of little boys. Little girls seemed already world-weary at eleven; but boys were still coltish and wide-eyed, and she loved them for that. Children had always given her such joy.

The Hill Queen

1966

Kinder Falls was named for the series of miniature cascades
that moved water from the hills to Lake Okisee, all of it carved
by glaciers millions of years before. It was German: children's
falls. The irony was lost on no one when the boy from South
Carolina went over the only waterfall in Schuyler's Creek and
died.

There's a boy went over the falls this morning, Dorie told Sam
the minute he came into the kitchen.

Oh God, Sam said. Do we know him?

Summer kid. From South Carolina, they said.

Sam sat down and looked at his hands. Turned them over.
Awful, he said.

Only fourteen.

Sam looked at his wife. Lines dug deep from mouth to jaw.
Wide forehead, thin lips. Huge bosom supported by a big,
round, belly. How he loved her. Put it out of your mind, Dorie.
Don't let it get you. I'm serious.

Schuyler's Creek is dangerous, she said. Too many kids
monkey around up there. They should close it off.

Sam kissed Dorie on the top of her head. This isn't our
tragedy.

I know. Dorie couldn't stop herself from conjuring it though.

She didn't want to see it, just couldn't not: a group of kids, fooling around, splashing in the water that spilled down into the shallow pool at the base of the falls. A shape, a boy, tumbling over the edge, and bucking at the air as he fell, and fell, to the rock below. Could have been any boy. Could have been one of her summer children. Could have been an omen. More bad coming. Her throat closed up and she had to sit down.

She thought like this—always the worst that could happen—and she couldn't stop herself. If she spied a deer on the side of the road, she imagined it leaping in front of her car and killing them both. If she went swimming far from the dock, she imagined a motorboat cutting her body to shreds. She saw disaster in the creeks, on bridges, in children in the crosswalk. And why not? If their Eli could die, then anything.

Dorie watched Sam back the Ford Falcon out of their drive and head to work. The dirt road—too close to the house— kicked up a cloud every time a car came or went; it was worse in the summer when the windows were open. The sun lit a tangle of her hair on the linoleum tile. She'd gotten her first gray too young, after Eli, and at sixty the last strands of brown lay hidden at the nape of her neck.

She glanced at the open newspaper Sam had left. There in the upper corner, filling a good quarter of the page, was a picture of Frances Price standing at a microphone at the town meeting. Dorie put on her glasses. Frances was concerned, it said, about methane leaking from the Epps's hastily dug wells. She was concerned, it said, about damage to the ground water. There had been a massive fire in Parker County, Texas, Frances said, from a gas well blow-out last year, and there was no guarantee the same thing wouldn't happen in Kinder Falls. Dorie was annoyed. How would Frances Price know anything about gas mining? Sam worked on the pumps at the drill site; if there was anything that could go wrong, he'd know. Dorie dog-eared the page with the photo of Frances. She'd ask Sam about it later.

Voices came bubbling toward her house. Her summer children, coming up the road! They were not her children, technically, of course. They were local kids—all cousins—who spent summers with their grandmother, Evelyn Dunn, in the yellow Victorian on the lake. She met them when they had stopped at her house to ask for a drink of water in early July, and she made them iced tea and let them pick her raspberries. Ever since, they came by once a week. Lee was the oldest at twelve, already trying out a swagger. Alice, the youngest, only five. Her favorite was the eight-year-old Caroline Epps, with creamy pink skin and long, white-blonde hair, a little doll. Dorie loved to entertain them. She'd spread her blue-checked cloth over the tree stump they used as a table. She served them sweet tea in tall glasses and cookies on a gold-edged plate. They called her the Hill Queen, and she let them think she was one. She had no idea what Mrs. Dunn thought, or even if she knew they were up here. She didn't care. She was giddy with the fullness of children.

They swarmed her, chattering. Dorie got a whiff of acetone from the oldest girl: nail polish. The younger boys were starting to smell acrid, where only last month they smelled of Ivory soap. The summer was flying. Her life was flying. She barely got the beans in this year; June had surprised her.

Chick-burr, chick-burr. Sweet whistling from above.

It's a scarlet tanager, she told the children. Look for him. He'd be up at the very top of the tree.

All the tender white faces craned upwards searching the beech trees that surrounded Dorie's home. Little birds, mouths open and chirping, the six of them. She treasured this time before braces, where teeth were allowed to grow crooked and gapped. Let this last, Dorie prayed. Let me have this.

Later that week Dorie spotted Frances coming out of Beezy's White Elephant with a small package wrapped in brown paper. She caught up with her.

Frances, did you study geology in college?

Dorie! I haven't seen you in a dog's age.

I'm wondering if you studied geology, Dorie said, because I saw that article in the paper. They're not poisoning the earth, Frances. Don't be dramatic. If something bad was going on out there, Sam would know.

He might not, Dorie. It's a sneaky business. And from what I've read and the people I've talked to out in Denver, we'll be stuck with their mess for decades. The access roads they built? Who's going to maintain those? And the fire in Texas—

Dorie rolled her eyes. People have been digging wells for centuries, Frances, and the ground hasn't exploded yet. What you were doing at that town meeting, it could cost people their jobs. She didn't like how her voice was sounding. Weak, complaining. She took a moment to compose herself. What about Sam and all the men who work out there? she said. We're depending on those jobs, Frances. I think you're letting the tail wag the dog.

Frances hugged her package. It's short-sighted, Dorie. What will Sam do when the wells are dry? There are people who aren't born yet who will suffer from problems those wells will leave us.

Oh, for God's sake, Frances. I have enough on my plate that I can't be worrying about 300 years from now.

Well, said Frances. Someone has to do something for the children coming up.

Tears immediately sprung into Dorie's eyes. She'd never been able to stop this, not now, not twenty-four years ago, not ever.

Frances clutched Dorie's hand. Oh, Dorie, I'm so sorry. I didn't mean to be hurtful.

The women looked off over each other's shoulders, embarrassed. Dorie broke the silence. What's in the package, Frances?

A butter dish, Frances said. You going to the Labor Day picnic?

Of course.

I'll see you there then.

As children they'd been friends, Frances and Dorie, although they had little in common. Frances was serious, Dorie a giggler. Even as a teenager Frances had the flat, businesslike face and wide shoulders that gave her an air of authority. She'd worked in the city clerk's office all her adult life, ordering carbon paper and staples and talking with men who needed marriage licenses and construction permits. Dorie, in contrast, had been wide-eyed and ample-hipped, a prize among the boys. She'd married Sam Fish and kept a vegetable garden to sell produce at a stand in front of her house on weekends.

Why can't you be more like Frances? Dorie heard her dead mother whisper, fingernails digging into the soft, tender part of Dorie's upper arm.

Labor Day already? Dorie thought. She'd pick up charcoal for the grill.

The Iroquois, it was said, lit fires at the end of summer to encourage the late harvest. Since the end of the nineteenth century, everyone with lakefront property on Okisee did the same. Now they bought safety flares, lined their beaches with them and lit them all at once on the night before Labor Day. The sounds of parties drifted across the water. Woodsmoke and sulfur filled the air. Children were allowed to hold sparklers, and motorboats skimmed the surface of the lake, their red and green lights mirrored in the water.

From their porch up on the hill, Dorie and Sam could see the whole of Okisee, necklaced in glittering red. The moon was barely there, a baby's eyelash.

Labor Day always makes me a little sad, Dorie said. She lay her head on Sam's shoulder. My summer children will go back to school next week; they won't have time for me.

I know, Sam said gently.

Eli would have liked to play with them, she said.

Yes, he would have, Sam said.

Course, my summer children weren't even a twinkle in someone's eye back then.

And Eli had been so much more than a twinkle, he'd been a galaxy. Four years old with a butterfly net chasing a jack-rabbit in the warm afternoon sun when the air smelled like honeysuckle and there were hours and hours to play before dark. The refrigerator repair truck driver, not thinking of little boys, did not see the tiny figure in the middle of the road. Dorie was in the side yard of their apartment on Dutch Street, downtown, pulling knotweed from around the fence, still talking to Eli, who'd been there only a moment before, and was gone so quickly that it took her days to comprehend.

Dorie and Sam moved out of the town of Kinder Falls to a small house on the hill that shouldered the lake, with few neighbors, fewer cars, and no refrigerator trucks. Dorie ate all of her curves away; her fat was a punishment she savored. They left the Congregational church, as they had no use for a God that had no use for them.

He was still with her, little Eli. A whiff of Vick's VapoRub made Dorie's fingers tingle with the memory of massaging his tiny chest. Morning glories were his eyes at birth; periwinkle then, brown by two. But most of all he was the lake. Dorie always saw Eli reflected in the water—a beautiful boy made of sunshine dancing on the surface of Okisee—and she'd reach out her arms, but he'd laugh and turn away, as if someone had called him. This was her guilt, which was always close.

The flares were burning down. Dorie sighed. Frances Price thinks you're ruining the earth with the drilling, she said.

It's a well like a million other wells, Sam said.

What if there's an accident?

There won't be.

What about explosions? Frances said that a gas well exploded in Texas. Killed a man.

That's ridiculous.

I thought so. I don't know where she gets her ideas.

Sam brightened. You making macaroni salad for the picnic?

I suppose. Everyone always asks for it.

The picnic grounds were covered with dry pine needles. Frances Price placed her perfect deviled eggs—pale yellow swirly mounds—next to Dorie's macaroni salad, sweaty with oil, its coarse-cut red pepper bits sagging.

Hello Frances, Dorie said, smiling with all her teeth. She swatted flies off the salad table. Across the grass she glimpsed Evelyn Dunn leading her daughter and grandchildren—Dorie's summer children—like ducks. Dorie tried to stop herself from looking at them but she couldn't. Mrs. Dunn's nylons glinted in the sun like the underbelly of a trout snapping bugs at dawn.

This is Helen, Frances was saying, holding the elbow of a short, dark-haired woman with thick eyebrows and beautiful teeth. Helen, this is Dorie.

Dorie took the woman's hand: porcelain skin. Pleasure to meet you.

And you too, Helen said, her voice joyful, eyes twinkling. Frances has told me oodles about her friends in Kinder Falls.

Dorie looked Helen in the eyes to check for sarcasm. Nothing but a cheery brightness.

Helen and I went to college together, Frances said, rearranging the dishes on the table.

How nice you've kept up all these years. Dorie said.

Why wouldn't we? Frances asked, head cocked.

Helen scooped up a swath of Dorie's skirt. What a beautiful dress, Dorie! I love those white flowers—what do you call them?

Dorie startled at the sudden waft of air on her knees. She was self-conscious. Queen Anne's lace, she said nervously. They're everywhere around here. A weed, really. Wild carrot. Why was Dorie talking so much? Oh, look, there's Sam. I came over to get a plate for him, so, well, it was nice to meet you, Helen. Hope to see you again.

You will! Take care, Dorie.

Sam was under a tree talking to the children's librarian, who wore a T-shirt emblazoned with an American flag and a peace sign. Dorie piled a paper plate full of macaroni salad and went to him.

Did you see Frances come through with her eggs? he asked hopefully.

Couldn't find them, Dorie lied. That table's crowded with everything you can put mayonnaise in.

They sat on folding chairs in the shade alongside the soprano section of the church choir, whose heads were bent together practicing their part for "Bread and Roses." Oak leaves lifted and settled, robins drifted above, and the people of Kinder Falls wove together like a pastel tapestry of floral dresses and light-colored shirts. The littlest children clung to legs, afraid of all the adults they didn't know, of the loud bursts of laughing, the sharp admonishments of mothers. Dorie's summer children were at the lake's edge, pressed, starched, and spotless, playing with sailboats attached to strings in the shallows and somehow not wet.

When you lose a child, Dorie thought, the world fills with things they would have loved, and this—the picnic, the grape soda, the sack races—Eli would have loved all of it. He would have been kind to the Manning's albino girl, maybe had a crush on the children's librarian, bought a used car from the Dowling's and fixed it himself when it stalled. Looking around, Dorie felt a calm in her heart where there was usually a wet knot.

Reverend Machover began: Dear Lord, hear our prayer. He stood under the town's oldest oak, a tree whose silver bark was cut deep with growth fissures and whose first branches were as high as the top of the picnic shed and reached wide across the scrubby field. The town's children sat in messy rows beneath him, ready to say the pledge. Their faces were alternately bored and astonished at this man, huge in their eyes, arms uplifted, sleeves flapping like bat wings, face round and white like a moon rising over their town, safe, good, right.

The oak dropped a few acorns in a breeze.

Frances bent close to Dorie's ear. It's amazing that this earth gives back after all we're doing to it, she said quietly. It's generous, don't you think?

The day after Labor Day, Dorie set out her checked tablecloth, emptied an ice tray into the bowl. She fixed her hair on top of her head—very Hill Queen-like, she thought—and listened with joy to the excited voices of her children coming up the road. School began again on Wednesday; that they would spend their last afternoon of summer with her made Dorie burst with happiness. She sang them a song in German she remembered her own grandmother singing, and they sang her an awful song about worms. The oldest boy said he had a lucky chain letter he'd like to send her, and she said she'd like nothing more. They tied thread to peanuts and hung them from the clothes rack for the chipmunks. The girls' knees got dirty and Dorie let them go inside to wash them off.

There's dead deer antlers in your house, said the tiny, pretty one, Caroline.

That's right, Dorie said lightly. My husband is a hunter, and that deer was a 12-pointer. He's quite proud of it.

The children were quiet. The littlest squirmed and tried to climb off her lap. Dorie held her tighter. Lots of people hunt deer around here, Dorie continued, trying to lift the mood.

My Grandpa Mitchell doesn't, Caroline said.

Dorie's tongue felt sticky. She couldn't think fast enough. Well, people are different, I suppose.

Nana! the littlest shouted, pointing at the road.

Dorie hadn't registered the car chugging up the hill. Despite the dust kicked up by tires, it was a spotless Cadillac Coupe Deville, champagne, all polished chrome and whitewall tires. It stopped in front of Dorie's house and a woman's tiny shoe emerged, high-heeled, open-toed. Her leg followed, shapely, stockinged. A navy skirt, white blouse, bowed and pearl-buttoned, a blue jacket. For all that clothing, she stood a diminutive five feet. She removed her sunglasses and took in the house, yard, children, Dorie.

Hello, Mrs. Dunn, Dorie said.

Mrs. Dunn smiled wanly. She opened the back door of the Cadillac. The children obediently filed toward the car. Mrs. Dunn placed a hand on the back of each child's neck as she shepherded them into the wide back seat. She looked past Dorie at the house and yard, with its outdoor antique wringer and broken snowplow attachment, the bushes Dorie had not yet had time to prune and the flowerbed of spindly black-eyed Susans.

Mrs. Dunn's gaze settled on Dorie, and for the first time in as long as she could remember, Dorie felt herself blush. Self-consciousness gradually turned to shame, then to anger as Mrs. Dunn continued to look at her. Her little house was a beat-up shack up on a hill where it was always hot and there was nothing but cows and hay and some electric fence to keep it all separate. Her baggy flower print dress with the gathers at the waist was lurid, and so were the veins that popped out behind her legs, as if you could see through her skin to what she was made of and how it all worked under there.

I'd no idea this is what they were up to, Mrs. Dunn said. I'm sure they've been a nuisance.

Oh no, Dorie said. Not the least bit.

Well, I'd rather they didn't spoil their dinner, Mrs. Dunn said, her smile forced. You understand.

Dorie nodded, fanning herself with a paper napkin. She understood perfectly.

You take care now, said Mrs. Dunn as she slid into the driver's seat. Her skirt didn't ride up, her legs came apart for only a brief moment, and her nylons made a quick swishing sound. She closed the door and said something to the children that Dorie couldn't hear. The oldest boy rolled up his window. The other children turned their heads forward, silent soldiers.

Dorie watched the Cadillac motor down the hot, rutted road, past the pasture and the creek head, barely a trickle leaking from an outcrop of rocks, past a lone man on a tractor far away, mowing hay. Big man in overalls, no shirt even though the sun was August-mean, skin tanned dark like a shadow under a straw hat.

After Eli, Dorie made herself sit on a kitchen chair in the middle of her garden every single day and look until she saw something beautiful. The buttery leaves of daffodils in the spring, the pink petals on her apple tree. Lipstick-y red berries, blue-eyed cornflower. She had wanted to teach the summer children this, her hardest-earned wisdom: how over time, if you're brave, beauty can soften loss. Now she'd never be able to. She'd been robbed again of joy, of children. She had let herself be shamed by a seconds-long gaze and a pair of seamless nylon stockings. Dorie went out to her garden, picked a ripe tomato and stuffed the whole thing in her mouth. Choke me, I dare you, she said. Choke me dead.

Fall lit up the hillsides with orange and yellow, November turned them a dull brown, and by February the ground was strewn with broken tree limbs from the ice storm that also tore up the Singer Sewing Machine store roof. Come spring, the year-round residents couldn't wait to be outdoors again. Potatoes and peas went into gardens, docks rolled out into the lake, patio umbrellas re-emerged at the snack stand, and Dorie was combing through the newspaper looking for work. Sam had dislocated his shoulder back in January, and Donny Epps had promised he could have the job back when he was better, but the stinker replaced Sam within a week. Next time a spot opens, he'd promised, you're first in line.

The want ads were always slim in the spring. Vineyards were mostly empty of workers, the tourist season hadn't started, and the only jobs available were the work of keeping the town going: caring for the old folks, filling potholes, serving school lunches. Dorie's only real experience outside her own home was taking care of her Uncle Harley. She'd been good at it.

The ad was bigger than all the others on the page: Wanted. Daytime help for invalid, 1–4 p.m. Must be willing to read aloud, be pleasant and kind. She called the number. She knew who it was.

Evelyn Dunn's Victorian had a weedless lawn that sloped to the lake. The property was landscaped with low rock walls and dahlias, dozens of dahlias, hundreds of dahlias, in August. At Christmas, each window was hung with a wreath and lit with an electric candle. There were at least twenty-four windows; Dorie had counted. The Dunns had a beautiful, gleaming white inboard motorboat. She associated the house with the ticking of the crank that secured the boat at twilight in the summer.

Mrs. Dunn! she said cheerily when Mrs. Dunn's daughter Thea led her into the bedroom. A stroke had rendered the left side of Mrs. Dunn's face useless, but her right eye was alert and suspicious. I'm so sorry, Thea, Dorie said quietly. Dorie sat next to the bed and patted Mrs. Dunn's lifeless hand. What are we reading? she asked. Mrs. Dunn's face turned the color of tarnished spoon.

The daughter handed over *Nicholas and Alexandra,* dogeared at page forty-seven. Dorie leafed through the book. Long chapters, small type. Of course, she said, closing the volume.

The stroke paralyzed most of her body, Thea said, smiling down at her mother, but Mama's mind is still bright. You'll start to figure out what some of her sounds mean. Read to her for a bit; she'll get sleepy and nap after a while. Feel free to get whatever you like from the kitchen. There are extra blankets in the cedar chest if she needs them. If you can't find anything,

Bea next door will come. She's good with mother. I'm usually back by four o'clock.

There were other instructions, but Dorie was focused on the helpless limbs that lay like twigs under Mrs. Dunn's comforter. Although her daughter had propped her mother against a mountain of pillows, the woman was already slumping to the side. Thea kissed Mrs. Dunn and left.

Well, aren't we a pair? Dorie said as she sat down next to the bed to read. Hard to believe we're both barely sixty; health is everything, isn't it? Well, let's get to it. Dorie read in a normal voice, then lowered her voice so that it was inaudible. Mrs. Dunn's right eye bulged with anger. So sorry, Dorie would say. Louder? How loud? Like this? Mrs. Dunn blinked against the sound and grimaced, annoyed. It was cruel of her, Dorie knew. She felt a tiny pang of guilt at the end of each afternoon when Thea thanked her so sincerely, and another on paydays, but she was accustomed to guilt.

Each time Dorie arrived and Thea left, Mrs. Dunn's eye would close and her breathing quicken. If she was a dog, Dorie thought, you'd say she was panting. One Friday, Dorie felt like talking.

Tell me, Mrs. Dunn, about the beautiful things in your room here.

Mrs. Dunn closed her eye.

Dorie picked up a pearl-handled hairbrush. Like this. Mrs. Dunn's eye flipped open. Is this real pearl? It's lovely. Remember when you came and took the children from my house? I do. That day is so clear in my memory. Dorie brushed the thin gray strands on Mrs. Dunn's head, so dry the air crackled each time she ran the bristles across the pale skull. You in your champagne Cadillac with your open-toe shoes and your suit. I suppose your grandchildren will come stay with you on the lake again this summer? I can't wait to see them all. Especially your youngest. Such a precious girl. Dorie cupped Mrs. Dunn's chin with one hand and brushed the hair back from her face. Mrs. Dunn's lips pulled back from her teeth with each stroke. You know what she told me once? She said she wished I was her grandmother. Ha. Isn't that funny? Me. She didn't mean it, of course. At least I don't think so. Who could really know what goes on inside a five-year-old's head? I can't say I do. My Eli was four when he left us. Of course, you know that. Everyone in Kinder Falls knows that. When Eli died, well, that was the worst it's ever been. You think you can't go on, but you do. You find a way.

Dorie dropped the brush on Mrs. Dunn's pillow and went to the closet. She ran her hands over the clothes, pulling out a sleeve here, a skirt, a scarf. So much silk! These are all so expensive! Dorie took a dress off its hanger and held it up to her body. What you learn to do is this, Mrs. Dunn. You look for joy in the smaller things, things that you *can* have. A healthy garden. Cookies. Children who visit, who keep you company. Why would someone take that away? Why would they, Mrs. Dunn? I think this dress would look lovely on me, don't you? It's such a beautiful green. Dorie stripped to her bra and underpants and stepped into the dress. Oh pooh, I can't zip this up at all, my bosom's too big, but doesn't the color suit me? She stood so that Mrs. Dunn had to look at the feathery stretchmarks that spread across both enormous breasts and made white tracks toward her stomach. Oh, don't close your eye, Mrs. Dunn. I want you to see how beautiful your dress looks on me. You'll never wear it again, so why shouldn't you get some pleasure out of seeing it on me?

Dorie spun in the green dress. It's so silky.

Mrs. Dunn's eye darted side to side.

Silky, silky, silky, Dorie sang.

The front door to the house opened. Dorie froze. Footsteps

came toward the bedroom, the door swung open, and Frances Price filled the frame. Dorie clutched the dress closed over her breasts, opening her mouth, then closing it, then opening it again. What are you doing here, Frances? Dorie's voice was small, like a child's.

Frances's eyes darted from Dorie to Mrs. Dunn. Delivering paperwork the daughter asked for, she said. What on earth are you doing, Dorie?

Dorie looked helplessly at Frances. Her eyes teared.

Okay, okay, Frances said. She touched Mrs. Dunn lightly on the shoulder. We'll be a minute, Mrs. Dunn. Why don't you rest a bit? Frances led Dorie from the bedroom and closed the door behind them. Let's go have some tea, you and me.

Frances found a robe on a hook in the bathroom and helped Dorie into it. Sit down, Dorie, she said, and tell me what was going on back there.

Dorie sat but she couldn't figure out a way to start a sentence. She tried, but her mind was a tangle. When she did speak, her voice came out in a whisper: She has so much, Frances.

Frances poured water in the teakettle and lit the burner. Oh stop, Dorie. We all have what we have and there's no good or bad to it. What you have, what she has, what I have, it's all the same. Good and bad, sadness and love, we all get those.

No, it's not that I'm talking about. She took away my children. Last summer. She came up the hill and took them.

Mrs. Dunn? Now you're not making sense. The teakettle whistled. Frances took it off the burner and poured water into their cups. Drink this, she said. It'll calm you.

My summer children, Frances. Her grandkids. They came every week to visit me. We had iced tea and cookies and the littlest crawled into my lap. I was the Hill Queen to them. We played games; it was delightful, I treasured them so. But she came up the hill in her champagne car and took them all away. Shamed me. She was awful, Frances. Dorie sat quiet for a long moment, gathering the fabric of the robe, then smoothing it. I know it was un-Christian, what I was doing back there, but she deserved it.

Honestly, Dorie, Frances said, crossing her arms.

Dorie's eyes darkened. Don't get sanctimonious with me, Frances Price. There's a lot you don't know. Today is Eli's birthday, for one. Yes, dead children have birthdays like everyone else. And every year I have to live through it.

Oh, Dorie, Frances said quietly. Eli was a joy. He'll always be—

I don't believe in God, Frances. And I don't believe in heaven. And don't tell me Eli will always be in my heart because until you've lost someone you really love, you have no idea what that does to you. Eli is not something to let go of because he's gone. He's still mine, and I still need to care for him because he lives in me, he's still a joy to me. The dead are so alive, so very alive, Frances. Grief gives you something to wrap your arms around. She shook her head. I should never have let him out of my sight. We should have put in a fence; the road was right there.

Oh, Dorie, you need to stop thinking like that.

I don't know how.

Frances took a big breath as if she was going to start a long speech but stopped herself.

The kitchen clock ticked loudly. Frances counted the ticks: thirty-five. She turned to look at Dorie. Why didn't you and Sam ever have another?

Sam wanted to. I didn't think we deserved another.

Frances caught her breath. You didn't think you deserved one? That's the most selfish thing I've ever heard, Dorie Fish. Of course you did. Maybe you'd rather punish yourself but honestly, Dorie. Didn't deserve one. My God. What about Sam? Did he?

There was a long silence.

Well, Dorie said. I guess you had that cooking in your head for a while.

Maybe I did, Frances said. She came up behind Dorie and wrapped her arms around the woman. Dorie covered Frances's hand with her own. Dry, warm, knotty. The two of them stood still, there in Mrs. Dunn's kitchen, with the afternoon sun lighting up the toast crumbs on the counter.

The truth is, Frances, I didn't think I could love another as much as I loved Eli.

Now that, I believe, Frances said. You loved Eli truly.

Now you, Dorie said. She squeezed Frances's hand and craned her neck around to look her friend in the eye. Why didn't you ever marry?

Frances gave an impish smile. Oh, I guess the right man never came around.

Well, that's nonsense. Maybe you're too particular.

Could be, Frances said. She picked up their teacups. How about you get dressed and go home to Sam. I'll clean up here. I'll tell the Dunn daughter you had a dentist's appointment.

Thanks, Dorie said. My clothes are back in her room. Would you?

Yes, of course. Frances went back toward the bedroom and returned with Dorie's skirt and blouse.

She asleep?

Out cold.

Thank goodness. You won't say anything about what I did, will you?

Never, said Frances.

Sam picked Dorie up in the Falcon. He had good news. Kinder Falls' water and sewer department was contracted to lay new pipelines from the lake to all the homes, which was approved by the citizen's board when some consumer group Frances Price had brought in discovered contaminated well water on Atkins farm over in Sugarton. Sam had been hired, full time, full benefits. Dorie didn't have to work for the Dunns anymore.

Dorie smiled and kissed her husband on the cheek. You deserve this, she said. I was done with Mrs. Dunn and her ninny of a daughter anyway.

Done with Dunn? Sam smirked.

Done and done with dummy Dunn.

He reached his arm around Dorie and pulled her next to him. She relaxed into his warmth.

It didn't gall Dorie that Frances had been right all along about the wells; Frances made wrongs right. Dorie admired that. They were cut of the same cloth, she and Frances. They were both essentially good women.

Mrs. Dunn died in late spring, and the news washed over Dorie like the smallest wisp of spider web. In her opinion, Mrs. Dunn's heart had stopped the day she took away Dorie's summer children. Only her brain had to die to finish it all.

That summer was warmer than usual, and Dorie took to swimming every day. Daughter Dunn had told her she could use their dock and the boathouse any time she wanted; the daughter had been grateful for Dorie's help with her mother. Dorie stood on the Dunn's dock in a florid red bathing suit with a ruffled skirt, tucking her hair into a rubber cap. She lowered herself into the lake. It was evening, when the water was warmer than the air. She closed her eyes and breathed in the smells. It was her bedrock, this lake, here, this Okisee shale and water, where she was born, and where all that she had earned, and built, and planted, lost, and loved, was. Where he could find her, their baby boy who she could always sense close by in the dusky phosphorescence. The point of life was not to be happy, Dorie thought; it was to be held. And she felt held by place, by light, perfectly balanced between water and air, between joy and pain. She cupped her hands under Eli's tiny body. Relax, she told him, I've got you. Spread your arms and legs; trust me. Let the water float you. I'll be right here. I'll always be right here.

If Eli

I run with a string tied to my heel, I'm a kite I'm a kite and the wind lifts me up and down below people in beds and on hammocks are squishing bugs and pressing buttons to turn lights on and off and they're cutting grass and cutting tangled fish lines and cutting grapes from stems and cutting a slice from the last peach

I come when the pink lies down under Mama's apple tree and when the sun holds me and when the leaves go red and when the water stops in ice I am always here

I am running-running under the clothesline, behind the fence, around the prickers, across the street careful, careful, dead squirrel flat on the road, shiny bottlecap, popsicle melting on the dirt, doors, stores, buttons, soap, brooms, pie and onions, Coca-Cola, pretty color tissue flowers, church, church, church, church, chugachugachugachuga train far away, one green house, two, basement smell of wet dirt, glass jugs full of dead flies, stone steps down-down-down, hot stones, running-running toward the water cool and sweet like icebox cake, alive like fireworks, seaweed floating like ribbons on the bottom

Pull the lake around me and wait for her

You'll Float

Caroline

Relax. Float your arms and legs—let them hang in the water, Della said.

No, I'll sink.

When she was thirteen, Caroline Epps had been allowed to go with her best friend Della, Della's dad, and his girlfriend to Lake Michigan for a week, which was such a huge expanse of gray water she couldn't imagine the other side. Her eyes stung and her teeth chattered; she had no body fat. She was irritated with Della, with her muscled torso and long legs that made her a natural swimmer, with her comfort in the frigid water that hugged Caroline like wet pants and smelled of dead fish. It was August, but Della said this was as warm as this lake ever got. It's too big to ever be warm, she said. And you won't sink. You'll float. Your head and chest float.

How could they? Caroline argued. They're the heaviest parts.

Trust me, Della said. Lay back and I'll hold you up.

Della held out her arms and Caroline lay back in them. She let her arms float out to the sides but she kept her muscles tight, a rigid starfish. She didn't want Della to know she couldn't swim yet.

Now relax. Seriously, Caroline, I've got you.

Caroline felt Della's arms supporting her, so she closed her eyes and opened her legs, let her head go, so that all she could hear was her breath tunneling in and out of her nose. The sun burned against her face and the sounds of the shore—gulls, kids, whistles—were muffled as if they were coming from another dimension. Her arms lifted and settled on the waves, her legs, too, and she suddenly had no idea how big she was, or where she was exactly, and it occurred to her that she may have already drifted far away from the beach where the lifeguard was. She opened her eyes in panic, flailing, and set her feet down, not in the deep, but in three feet of water inside the swim ropes. Della was laughing, yards away, a silhouette with the sun over her shoulder.

See? Della said.

Caroline hated her and loved her all at once.

Everything Wants to Be

1981

Now they were twenty-three. Della's apartment was at the end of Van Noyes Street outside of Kinder Falls, a faded brick apartment building next to a stagnant cow pond. Della had her hand in the disposal, feeling around for whatever had fallen in and was making that awful noise.

Sometimes you want something so bad you can make it real, Della was saying. You have to see it, like in your mind. Murph does it. Before he buys a scratch card, he closes his eyes and lets a number come to him. From the universe, he says. And he waits until there are five of them, then he writes them down and those are the numbers he plays. He's won twice. Big money, too, not ten or twenty dollars.

Caroline rolled her eyes. You really think that works?

You have to believe it works. It comes from your subconscious. Like you can shape reality with your mind.

I'm guessing Murph plays so many scratch cards the odds are he'll win once in a while.

Maybe. Or maybe there's a lot we don't know yet. You're the big college grad. Isn't it true that the smarter you are, the more you don't know?

Caroline couldn't tell if Della was making fun of her or not. They were already two vodka lemonades in. The afternoon was coming on humid and the bugs tapped against the kitchen screen door like fingernails.

It's what I do for Murph, Della said, after a while. Want something so bad you make it real. I picture him walking. In my head, he's walking up those back stairs. If it hadn't snowed—

None of us knew it was going to happen, Dell.

It was me, Caroline. It was my weight that did it.

It was the ice.

It was me.

There it was. There it always was. The biggest blizzard of 1977, senior year of high school. A chicken fight in the snow. Della on Murph's shoulders, Caroline on Pete's. Running at each other and tangling up their arms and pulling until one went over. The asinine, gleeful look on Murph's face, Della egging him on, pressing her heels into his ribs like he was a race-horse. Of course she had a crush on him. Always had, since middle school. Murph's boot hitting a patch of ice under the snow and him going down straight-backed trying to protect Dell from hitting the ground, and there was a snap that they all felt in the bottom of their stomachs. A sound they'd never heard before from a person, something like what happens when you twist a chicken leg from a thigh, but louder and wetter. Murph twitched and made sickening noises, and Caroline screamed for Pete to call an ambulance while Della held Murph's head, apologizing to the head, that didn't seem like it was connected to the rest of Murph, the angle he was at.

The angle.

You heard it break, Caroline. But I felt it.

It was an accident, Dell.

Della colored in black triangles on a paper towel. I don't believe in accidents, Caroline. You gotta come to the place with me next time I go. He asks about you sometimes. He talks like normal now.

I will, Dell. Next time for sure.

He lights up when I come into his room.

I'm sure he does.

Don't patronize me. Who lights up for you, Caroline?

What the hell is that supposed to mean?

Sorry. Dell's eyes were bright. She laughed. When we had that twentieth birthday party for Murph, it was awesome. With that old guy outside his window playing the trombone, and the fireworks. And he gave me a cake when Pete and I divorced, a happy divorce cake. Della laughed. Only Murph would think of that.

The buzzing in the fields was coming in waves. Cicadas, desperate in the first real heat of June. Caroline and Della watched the heat gather, drinking and thinking.

The house is too quiet, Della said at last. I don't like it. Della's three-year-old, Angela, was at Pete's for the night.

Caroline sighed. Come on, Dell. We never get a chance to hang out, just us. She lifted the kitchen curtain and stared across the grassy field at the weathervane on Frances Price's shingled garage roof. Still as a heat-stunned cow. It was pretty much always still, she thought. She licked the back of her arm to see if she could feel any movement of air on her skin. Nothing. God what an awful part of the country this was.

A car backed out of the garage, Ms. P. on her way to town. Caroline watched the gray Toyota drive past, 10 mph under the speed limit. She could see Ms. P. inside, her white head like a fuzzed out dandelion.

Ms. P. names her orchids, you know, Caroline said. Human names like Judy and Bob, but she won't let me touch them. She has a glass room just for flowers.

So, what does she pay you for?

Vacuuming the rugs, emptying the trash, stuff like that. I think mostly she's lonely.

I don't imagine you want to be cleaning houses as a career, am I right, Caroline?

It's only for the summer.

Then what?

I don't know. Dell and I might move to Chicago, on the lake.

You have a lake right here.

The lake there is bigger.

That it is.

And I like the idea of no one knowing who I am.

Is that so awful? To live around people who know you?

Who think they do.

I see.

It feels so small here.

Not to me, Caroline. Frankly, it feels vast.

Ms. P.'s car motored over a small rise and disappeared. Such a sad, gray car. Ms. P. really misses her Helen, Caroline said, pulling the curtain closed.

Della's head swayed back and forth to Bob Marley on the cassette player. Yeah, I bet. Helen was the nice one; it's too bad she died first. Della looked up at Caroline, her eyes narrowing. You know, Caroline, you missed things too. You missed Angela being born. Murph's twentieth. You missed everything big.

I had school, Dell.

You left us.

No. I went to college.

You didn't come see me until Angie was already two months old.

I came home at Christmas. Let's not do this, Dell.

Oh, we are definitely doing this. Because you don't get it, Caroline. It's about loyalty. It's what being a friend is. About being there for somebody, no matter what. Murph. Me, even Pete. We were your friends.

Friends, Caroline thought. There were months she didn't hear from Della, times when she'd call and Della wouldn't pick up. Then, days later, a bogus excuse. Our phone was off the hook. Pete forgot to tell me. And every single time it hurt.

I'm here now, Dell.

Yeah, because you don't know what else to do.

Screw you, Dell.

Screw you, Caroline.

The two of them sat quietly for a long time, heads full of vodka and hearts thumping with every ragged bass note emanating from the tape deck.

You want to watch some TV? Della said.

Sure.

The land rolled away into the distance, burnt yellows and ochres bordered with what Frances Price knew were decades-thick brambles. Stunted cherry, parched crabapple. The fields made you look wide, but never up, with the vineyards in neat, horizontal lines. She had driven into town to do errands: market, dry cleaners, library. She stayed at the library for a long while looking for—what?—a book written by someone like her, but one step further along, someone who could tell her what was next, what to do when the light goes out of your life but you still have years to get through. She ran her finger over the spines in the Spirituality section. Nothing. She felt the librarian watching her, pretending not to. People in Kinder Falls thought she was cold, she knew that. She was not cold; she was efficient. It's what you need to be as town clerk. She'd filed their licenses and permits, registered them as voters and ran their elections. She didn't have time to be their social worker and friend. She'd done what she could—gone to their store openings and funerals and Fourth of July celebrations, but always with Helen.

Helen.

The library closed but there were hours to kill before bed-time, so Frances used her old key to unlock the side door of the town hall and slipped inside. She walked the corridors enjoying the echo of her heels on the tile. Each wooden door had a nar-row window through which she could glimpse a vertical slat of the office within. Dull furniture, unemptied trash cans, army green metal file cabinets. This used to be her kingdom. She thought she would love retirement; she didn't. It was calming to her now, to come here after hours and check that the doors were locked, the community bulletin board neatened up, out-dated notices weeded out. Hand-lettered signs that said "No Drill No Spill" had gotten buried under notices for pet sitters and free firewood. Annoyed, she re-pinned them on top of the others in the center of the board.

As she passed by the plate glass door of the Registry of Deeds, she swore she saw an old woman standing in the hall-way covered with birds. But it was the children's spring art contest winners reflected behind her, of course.

Everything okay, Ms. Price?

It was Randy, the custodian. The man reeked of cigarettes. Frances smiled at him and showed him the balled-up flier. Just trying to be useful.

Me too, he said, gesturing to the floor buffer parked at the end of the hallway. He stood awkwardly, hands in his pockets for a long moment. I haven't had a chance to say yet, Ms. P., but I'm really sorry about Helen.

Oh, thank you, Randy. That's very kind.

Helen, Frances thought, whose eyes would light up when the hibiscus petals spread wide in the afternoon sun, even at the end, when she was a tangle of bones sunk into the couch cushions, barely a shadow. *Flowers—are such—whores* she'd whisper, her breath coming in bursts. Ms. P. laughed softly.

I miss her every day, Randy. It's hard to get used to, after nearly twenty years together.

I imagine so, Ms. P.

It felt oddly intimate, Frances thought, the two of them alone in the darkening town hall. You'll think me crazy, Randy, but I thought I saw someone behind me, just now. It was only a reflection.

That happens a lot in here, Randy said. Something about the light and how everything echoes when the building's closed up. He looked over his shoulder, then back at Frances, and lowered his voice. I see people who used to work here running in and out of their offices, like they did before. Even ones who are dead. It never lasts, though; it's a quick flash, then nothing. I've gotten so used to it that it doesn't bother me. Maybe it's because of how much time I spend alone. I don't mind the ghosts.

Ghosts. Ha. Are you lonely, Randy?

I wouldn't say so. You, Ms. P.?

Yes, I'd say I am. When you lose the person you love, you lose track of who you are; you need to figure out a whole new *thing,* you know, a new way of being in the world. But at my age, what am I going to do? Take up tennis? A cloud blotted the light from the windows. Frances squinted at Randy, half-smiling. I thought you were going to stop smoking.

I tell people that, but honestly, Ms. P., it's my greatest pleasure.

Frances drove home and parked in the driveway. A faint light shone from her kitchen; she'd forgotten to turn off the pantry switch. She'd left the garage door wide open as well, and her Persian throw rugs lay in a pile on the grass; she'd meant to lay them out in the sun. She should bring them in but she couldn't move. She sat in her car and looked at the house. How quiet it would be inside, how empty. Where did you go, Helen? Frances wondered. Where specifically, as in where are the parts of you that escaped the crematorium? Are you floating in the air, cancer-free, pure energy—negative charges, positive charges— looking to join with others the way hydrogen finds oxygen? Do you have to lose your body to find that kind of perfect pairing? So many things are free from bodies. Does water love? Sound? Wind? Frances liked the idea of Helen having a charge; even if it was invisible, you could feel it, it was there.

She looked up at her garage, where the ivy was snaking under the shingles. She'd asked Caroline to cut it back, as it would only get worse. Why does everything want to be where it shouldn't? The shears had gotten so stiff and heavy she couldn't work them anymore. She stared down at her hands. They were veiny, but from age, not effort. Although age was a sort of effort.

Frances put the car in reverse, backed out of her driveway and drove through the impossible green of soybean fields at sunset, through the acres of rolled hay. Above her there was an expanse of colorless sky, a dome. Caroline was wrong, she thought. It wasn't small here; it went on forever. The Toyota rose over swells, dipped in hollows, floated through the twilight, driving itself. Her fingers felt odd on the wheel, as if they were fuller than the fingers she knew she had, fingers encased in fingers. She glimpsed a wildebeest grazing by the roadside, or maybe it was an antelope or a gazelle, and it whispered for her to come closer and she did and closed her eyes for a moment because it was so peaceful and she was so tired, and there was Helen, kissing her on the lips, and Helen was so young that Frances worried it wasn't Helen at all. Her eyes popped open. She jerked the wheel hard to the right in panic. To her horror the car skidded off the road and down an embankment, bumping over rocks and tearing through the underbrush, and Frances screamed and screamed until the car stopped itself in a ditch and she felt the stickiness of her own blood on her face and a sharp pain in her chest. She closed her eyes and concentrated on taking long, slow breaths.

The sound of the collision echoed across the fields. An ambulance arrived within ten minutes and took Frances to the hospital, where she received stitches for her forehead and was told she'd broken two ribs.

We're going to need to keep you here for a few days, the nurse said. Would you like me to call someone?

Frances lay back on her pillow and winced. Yes, please, she said, defeated. I need you to call Caroline Epps for me.

Frances looked at the bruises on her arms, touched the bandage on her forehead. She'd been driving that road for fifty-six years. She knew that road, knew its stop signs and telephone poles. It was as if Kinder Falls was kicking her out the way the ground heaves shards of glass in the spring. Her niece Adria was probably right. It was time to move on, be safe, live smaller.

Caroline and Della were in the kitchen, and Caroline said they should eat something so Della grabbed a box of vanilla wafers from her cupboard. Whoa, she said. Look out the window. The bugs are insane tonight.

This whole town is insane, Caroline said. She took a handful of cookies.

Remember, Della said quietly, when we went to see Murph that first time and his mother was there? Do you remember what she said? She said that if I wasn't such a fat pig, Murph wouldn't have broken his neck.

Murph's mother was crazy back then, Dell. She didn't mean it.

I was a fat pig.

You were not.

Della turned away. You don't know this, Caroline, but the biggest fear you have when you're a mom is that you'll be separated from your kid. They'll be kidnapped or die. But not Murph's mom. She's got her kid forever. It's worse.

Caroline slipped an arm around her friend's waist. Forget Murph's mother, Dell.

Della rolled out of Caroline's arm and walked to the fridge. When Angela comes home, I'm buying her everything she wants, she said. You never know what's coming at you. She took out a bag of frozen peas and held it to her head. You should try this; it really cools you down.

The phone in Della's bedroom rang. She threw the bag to Caroline and went to answer it.

Sounds like Ms. P. found you, Della called. It's her.

Caroline hurried into the bedroom.

Ms. P. wanted Caroline to lock the house and shut the garage door. Something about throw rugs. Caroline promised she would. When she came back to the kitchen, Della was putting on her shoes.

I'm itching to get out of my skin crazy tonight, Caroline. Can you drive?

Caroline and Della rode north on 38 toward The Drifters Pub. The moon was fuzzed out in the sky and their headlights lit up front yards filled with rusted things, as if the whole county was out working when a rain came and seized up every moving part. Detached snow ploughs, bedsprings, engine blocks, hubcaps. Trailers planted too close to the highway, wooden porches held up with 2x4s. Broken things from when they were kids: clothes drying trees, seesaws.

You and Della have been friends a long time, haven't you, Caroline?

Yeah. We used to read each other's minds.

And now you don't?

She's different. It's the kid, I think.

Or maybe you're different now.

I guess. It's just—

What?

I don't know.

What don't you know?

What I feel about her. What I want.

Do you know how I knew I loved Helen?

How?

I saw green flecks in her eyes. To everyone else, her eyes were brown.

I mean seriously, how did you know?

I am serious. I slowed down enough to see her. She was stunning.

Caroline pulled into the Drifter's lot and parked next to a pair of Harleys.

Good times, Della said, smiling. Caroline's stomach tightened.

The walls of the bar were still draped with Christmas bulbs and the bottles behind the bar sparkled in the light shot from a tiny mirror ball left over from last New Year's Eve. Inside, the kitchen door slammed open and a woman in a tank top with ham-sized biceps ran a tray of fried cheese sticks through the crowd. "Abomination" was tattooed across the back of her neck.

Sweet Jesus, look at those arms, Della said, stepping back.

Two guys in boots and black T-shirts were hunched together

at a table near the bar. They could have been Vikings, Caroline
thought, with the sheer bulk of their bodies. Dark jeans, tat-
toos, hair you knew stunk of sweat. Guys, Caroline knew, who
did their best performances for each other; girls were frosting.

Caroline and Della ordered more vodka and lemonade, and
within the first half-hour Della had flirted her way to the guys'
table and Caroline had made up new personas for them: Bunny
and Barb. Bunny and Barb kept up with the drinks, with the
stories, until Drifters closed, and it was so much fun to be back
doing crazy things with Della that Caroline told the guys she
knew a fancy place where the owner was gone, and they could
still party.

The one called Big Red found the bourbon in Ms. P.'s liquor
cabinet. He plugged in Helen's radio and Creedence came on
loud. And then Della was dancing to "Born on the Bayou,"
one hand holding a cocktail glass full of booze and one twirl-
ing over her head as she gyrated in the middle of the living
room. The carpet swam in Caroline's gaze, its luscious red and
gold pulsing with the bass notes from the radio, Helen's hand-
thrown bowls jittering on glass shelves. Caroline heard something break in the kitchen, and there was the other guy, Stitch,
standing in the mess of a broken mayonnaise jar, thick-necked
like a stallion, eating a roast beef sandwich. He turned to her,
mouth full. Bleary-eyed, she imagined she saw Ms. Price's
pinched white face peering at her from the window.

Come on, dance, I love this song, Caroline heard Della say.

When Caroline got back to the living room, Big Red was
slumped on Ms. P.'s couch, his legs spread wide, the inner
thighs of his jeans rubbed to a threadbare pale blue. His hair
was matted with sweat where his cap had been, with a fat red
line across his forehead. The skin on his neck was scarred like

marbled steak and the muscles in his forearms tensed as he clutched his glass.

I'd rather watch you dance, he said. In fact, I'd rather watch both of you dance. Together. The smile was gone from his eyes, his mouth drawn into a tight, twitching line as if he was chewing the flesh on the inside. Come on, Bunny, dance for me. You too, Blondie.

Della grabbed Caroline by the hands and made a few drunken steps forward and back, swing-dance style. Caroline tried to keep up but her head felt like it was going sideways and her feet were clumsy. The room spun, and Caroline held onto Della and buried her head in Della's shoulder, feeling Della's neck pulse on her temple, feeling their breasts mashed together, the dampness of sweat on their shirts. She let her body sink into Della's and closed her eyes to disappear the men, the couch, everything but Della. Della tried to wriggle out of her arms, but Caroline held tighter. Big Red whistled a low, long note.

Della's head snapped up. She shoved Caroline away.

Aw, come on, Stitch said, standing in the kitchen doorway, chewing. Don't stop now. He was a stretched-tight wiry kind of guy, all spark and muscle.

We don't feel like dancing anymore, Della said, running her hands through her hair.

I'm asking as nice as I can, Big Red said.

And I'm telling you I don't feel like it, Della said.

The flirt was gone from her voice. This, Caroline knew, was the ferocious Della, a Della who would kick these guys in the nuts without a second thought and damn the consequences.

Bunny, let's get some air, Caroline said.

Big Red rose slowly from the couch, eyes on Della. He was a monster of a man, built like a boiler.

Seriously, Bunny, I really need air.

Della didn't move, locked her eyes on Big Red's, daring him, until he was inches from her face. Dance, he said.

Della met his stare, a sneer on her lips. No, asshole, she said.

Red took a fistful of Della's hair and yanked her head back. She clawed at him, tearing at his grip. He locked his other arm tight around Della's waist, and she mule kicked him with all her strength. Red let out a holler. Caroline backed up against the fireplace, one eye on Stitch, one on the poker leaning against the grate. In one quick move she grabbed the poker and slammed it hard at Big Red's knees. He buckled and crashed to the floor with a roar. She took Della by the arm, shoved past Stitch, and ran across the yard to the back of the garage, her heart pounding. She pushed Della down into the giant hostas and crouched next to her with the poker gripped like a bat. The back door slammed. Caroline and Della slid down as far as they could into the shadows.

Stitch stared out into the fields beyond the Price property and scratched. I don't see them out here, Red.

Screw 'em, Big Red hollered from inside. Those girls are gone.

Yeah, I think you're right, Stitch said. Minutes later Big Red limped out of the house. The two men kicked the bikes into life and rode off. The rumble of their engines accelerated, then faded.

Della stood up and brushed the mulch off her thighs. What the hell am I doing? she said. We're not dumb kids anymore. I'm a mom for God's sake. I can't be getting into this kind of shit.

It's not us, Della. It's this place, these people. It's small and stupid.

What?

Seriously, Dell. If we don't get out of here we're going to be stuck forever, crippled like Murph. Only not our bodies. Our minds. Caroline couldn't stop the words from coming; she'd said them so many times in her head. Della, listen. I mean this. We could move. We could go to Chicago, you, me, and Angela. The lake is so big there, remember? We can get jobs, an apartment, do anything we want. We could get out of here. Let's do it, okay?

Della swatted at the mosquitoes clinging to her bare skin. Her face was twisted. A cripple? That's how you think of Murph? It was your idea, Caroline, the chicken fight. If you didn't strong-arm us into going out in the snow, Murph would be fine, and who knows how our lives would be different. But no, you were bored. Let's go outside. It's snowing, it'll be fun. And everyone always wants to do what princess Caroline wants. You're a spoiled brat. You ruined everything.

That's bullshit. What happened to Murph wasn't my fault and it sure as hell wasn't yours. It was an accident. Seriously, Della, get over it, or you're going to die in this shithole.

Shithole? This is my *home*. My parents are here. Angela's dad is here. Murph is here. I'm making a life for myself. What have you got, Caroline? Where are your college friends? Why don't you have a real job? Why are you even here?

Far away, over the trees and past the cornfields, it was dawning blue.

Caroline's voice was small and quiet. I've got you, Dell. She looked up into Della's face, but Della's eyes were dark shadows.

No, Caroline, you don't. You don't have me. And if you hate this place so much, and we're too stupid, too crippled, then go. Go. Get your shit together and go. Her voice softened. I'm never going with you, okay? Not to Chicago, not anywhere.

Caroline stared out at a line of trees bordering the fields, a dark scar in the growing light. Tears wouldn't come; they backed up and hurt.

You sure? she said, in a tiny voice.

Della sighed. Grow up, Caroline.

Caroline watched Della walk away, ghost-like in the pre-dawn gray. She looked over at Ms. P.'s house. Shit, she thought.

Fog hung low in the fields; everything was wet. Caroline breathed in the damp air, thick with decomposing leaves and rotting logs; everything busy becoming something else. She scanned the sky; the last of the night clouds lazed like milky X-rays of body parts. An unsettled feeling swarmed over her, a pressure more than a chill. In the haze rising off the grass, an army of beasts was taking shape. She was mesmerized by the sight, knowing full well what she was looking at and not knowing at all. Then the sun fully crested and gilded the graceful backs of a few dozen cows as they grazed.

I don't know what I'm doing, Ms. P.

You'll figure it out.

How can you say that?

You're not stupid, Caroline. Stop mooning around and move on.

Where?

Throw a dart. I don't know.

I can't. Not alone.

You'll find people. And eventually, someone. And when you do, don't let a moment pass without knowing how lucky you are.

Okay.

Don't okay me. I mean it.

Ms. P.'s house was trashed. There was mayonnaise smeared across the kitchen tile, a busted cantaloupe in the sink, an orchid snapped from its stem, a shattered lamp. The bathroom was sopping wet and the couch smelled like ass. Caroline filled a bucket and began to scrub. Kitchen, bathroom, bedrooms, flower room. She crawled over every inch of wood floor and marble tile, digging out caked-on crap with her fingernail. She cleaned up the glass, the carpet sullied with mud, erasing, erasing, erasing. The morning brightness stabbed her temples when she dragged a bag of trash down to the cans behind the house and hoisted it in.

She went to Della's apartment, but Della wasn't home. Caroline let herself in and sat at the kitchen table to wait. It wasn't long before Della showed up with Angela, who ran past Caroline, deliriously calling out the name of all her things. Hello bed! Hello book! Hello rug!

I picked her up a little early, Della said. She hates being away from home.

I can see that, Caroline said. I just came by—

I know.

Della walked Caroline to her car and they stood side by side, looking out at the acres of corn coming up, not yet a foot high. Della brushed her hand against Caroline's. Their fingers interlocked, briefly, then released.

Caroline drove to the hospital first. Ms. P. was sleeping. She quietly set the house key on the bed table. Ms. P.'s face looked peaceful. Folds of powdery white flesh fell away from her chin and tiny bumps dotted her eyelids. Her brows were all but gone, just a few bristles of light hair. Her earlobes hung low, stretched from decades of heavy jewelry. Her eyes opened.

How are you feeling Ms. P.?

Like dog's dinner, frankly. Ms. P.'s color had washed to soft beige, with dark bruises where the blood had pooled in her forearms. She reached out and clutched Caroline's arm. Caroline, I saw Helen.

Ms. P.'s skin was nearly see-through, and Caroline tried not to look at the bloated veins where blood chugged away across Ms. P.'s temples, or the stringy tendons under the skin of her hands.

She was there, on the road, Ms. P. said. She came to me, but then I wasn't sure it was her and she disappeared. Helen was looking for me; but I didn't believe it, and I lost her.

Caroline bent down close to Ms. P. If Helen came to find you once, she whispered, she'll come again. She'll find you.

Ms. P. reached up and patted Caroline's head. Hair too shiny, too yellow, she thought, like a chick embryo. A boxy woman in a bright red raincoat barged into the room and sat down with a whoosh of talc-scented air. Ms. P. folded her arms and smiled. My niece Adria, she chirped, as if announcing a bingo win. Adria, this is Caroline.

We know about the house party, Adria said, her lip curling in disgust. Neighbors heard it. I could call the police, you know.

Oh please, don't. I'm so sorry, Caroline said, not knowing which woman to look at. It was my fault. I tried to clean as best I could. Please, I'll pay for anything they broke. I'm really sorry.

Ms. P. patted Caroline's hand. I don't need all those things anyway. The orchids are a pain in the ass.

They were valuable, Adria said, unsmiling.

They're only plants, Adria, Ms. P. said. It's not like you can't get more.

When can you go home, Ms. P.? Caroline asked.

Thursday. But Adria wants me to come back to Rochester with her. Look for a condo, maybe. Ms. P. smiled cattily at Adria. If I can fit. Adria drives a Volkswagen.

Adria rolled her eyes. She shouldn't be alone, she said. It's dangerous out here, so far from everything. Small town doctors. Bad roads. It's not safe. Obviously.

Is there anything I can do for you, Ms. P.?

Adria is here now. She'll take care of everything. Ms. P. flicked her hands toward the door. You can go now, Caroline. Shoo!

Three hundred and twenty dollars and a Mastercard. Enough to get started, Caroline thought. She said her goodbyes to her sweetly baffled grandfather, her sullen mother. She drove past the Pentecostal church, the Church of the Seventh Day Adventist, the White Elephant shop, and the new CVS onto the two-lane where car exhaust had dulled the greenery to olive. She went past above-ground pools and propane tanks, prefab structures that could be schools or hospitals or electrical supply warehouses, out past old barns stripped to bare planks, past the Dairy Bar, past the fake windmill whose blades, for once, were turning. Storm coming, Caroline thought, or maybe it was Kinder Falls pushing her away, urging her onward at last. By the time she got to Buffalo the rain pounded her windshield and for the next two hours Caroline's hands were cemented to the wheel. Cars flew past sending up sheets of water. The radio played staticky announcements of candidates for police chief and recipients of Elks Club medals. She kept going, through Erie and along the lake, through Ohio and Indiana into Illinois, to Chicago, Lake Shore Drive, Roosevelt Road. Buildings rose like rockets around her. Caroline felt a yearning so raw it was like her chest was split open and her sides pinned back. Her whole body was agape, wanting something so big she couldn't find the edges of it. That's how big she felt now. Lake Michigan big. She drove along the endless shore, buoyed by speed, by the lights of hundreds of tiny windows. A sizzle ran up her spine. She felt achingly alone. So this is it, she thought. How everyone begins.

Fourth of July

1981

Mac & Neil

It was hardly a new beginning. Mac had been discharged from the army four months ago, but he still didn't have a job, and he was living in his childhood bedroom. From his beach chair in the backyard he could see Neil Morris, slouching against a ladder while his father strung white lights on the forsythia bushes between their two yards for his annual Fourth of July party. Neil was a high school French teacher now. Or had been, until the principal stepped into Neil's classroom on the day he decided to answer his students' questions about sex, and the principal saw the word "fellatio" written on the blackboard. That still made Mac laugh when he heard it.

The temperature was closing in on eighty degrees, and Mac's T-shirt was soaked through. Mac and his buddy Little Steven had pulled their chairs onto the strip of shade cast by Mac's house. Little Steven had been at Mac's since the night before as his girlfriend, Beth, had thrown him out. Again. It wasn't that he couldn't keep a job, Little Steven told Mac, it was because weird things kept happening to him. How could he have seen that after he poured the sidewalk and headed to town for lunch, only for an hour or so, okay, it was a little longer maybe, that a whole herd of Canada geese would walk through the wet cement while he was gone. So when his boss stopped by to check on him and saw all those webby footprints in the fresh cement, Little Steven was out of a job and now out of a home, at least until Beth cooled off.

I should call Beth and see if she's calmed down, Little Steven said.

Mac flipped the cap off his beer. I never can figure out what she sees in you.

She doesn't have much choice, Little Steven said. Kinder Falls is kind of fished out.

Big Al entered the backyard and angled his ass over an empty chair.

Where'd you come from? Little Steven said.

Your mama's house. Hey Mac, you know that Korean store near the post office?

Yeah.

Did you know they sell money that you burn?

Why would you burn money? Little Steven asked. That's stupid.

Spirit money. Asians burn it to honor their dead parents, Big Al said, to send it to them. Or to ask the gods for something. I got you some, Mac. You can do it for your dad.

Mac took the delicate paper bills. Thanks.

Little Steven snorted. Burning money. I don't think so. How do you even know that?

I know lots of weird shit, Big Al said. Like when a crocodile kills something, it buries the thing in the river bottom to soften it up. But then it looks up to the sky like it's asking for forgiveness.

No one could know that, Mac said quietly. He leaned his head back against the house and watched Neil.

Big Al took out a cigarette and was trying to strike a kitchen

match on the zipper fly of his jeans. You know the well water
on the farms up on the hill turned black as coal when they first
started drilling? You know they used to break up the rock with
Indian beads and nutshells?

Little Steven was stuck on the Korean store money thing.
Why not stick the money in their coffin? Why do you have to
burn it?

Big Al gave up on the match and pulled out his Bic. He
clicked it and the flame sparked. Fire purifies.

And that, my large friend, makes no sense, said Little Steven triumphantly. If fire purifies, then anyone who goes to
Hell, which is famously fiery, would get purified and bounce
right back up to heaven.

Hell isn't real, Steven, Big Al said.

Tell that to Beth.

Mac sighed. Weren't you going to call her?

Yeah. Little Steven stood up but the beach chair stuck to
his backside, so Big Al had to hold it while Steven wiggled free.

They'd all turned twenty-six this year. Little Steven was
thick-thighed and sweaty, not little at all, wearing size thirteen
shoes and a 3XL T-shirt, but he had to be Little Steven because
of the Boss. Big Al was rightly named. It was Mac who looked
out of place. He was slight and wound tight like the inside of a
golf ball. Spent 1979 in the Korean DMZ with the 2nd Infan-
try patrolling the Southern Barrier Fence. Quiet until December, when they stumbled into a North Korean minefield in
heavy fog: one killed, four wounded, took five days to recover
the body. Mac was discharged within a year and came home,
but he couldn't settle in.

You got bug spray? Little Steven asked. These midges are
driving me nuts.

They're no-see-ums, Big Al said.

Check under the sink in the kitchen, Mac said.

Mr. Morris climbed down, moved the ladder to the shed that sat at the back edge of the yard. Neil handed him a string of lights to run along its eave.

Isn't that shed on your property? Little Steven asked Mac.

Yeah, Mac said. Morris took it over when dad died.

He just took it?

Pretty much. Moved his junk in there. Mom didn't care.

That's not right, Little Steven said.

I guess.

So, what's in there? Big Al asked.

Old bottles, mostly. Glass. Stuff he collects.

People can't take property that's not theirs, Little Steven insisted. It's the principle of the thing.

It's nothing, Mac said. Forget it.

You should take it back, Little Steven said.

Mac rubbed the knot in his neck. Did you find the bug spray?

Oh, Little Steven said. I forgot.

Mac's backyard and the Morris's were indistinguishable: same crabapple trees, same patchy grass, forsythia hedge between the two. When they were kids Mac and Neil could jump over it, but now it was an untended mass of stringy branches that was taller than both of them.

Mac drank his beer and watched Neil loading boxes into the shed. Fireworks. Mr. Morris set them off over Okisee Lake as the big finale of the party. Crossette stars, comets, skyrockets, palms, and willows. Even firecrackers: Lady Fingers and Black Cats. Mac hated them all. Any loud bang sent crickets crawling under his scalp, dried out his mouth, and pulled a black curtain over his brain. It hadn't always been like that, but it was now. If you really could burn money to ask the gods for something, Mac thought, he'd shoot off every firework in that box to have never seen Korea. And fuck the Z.

By five o'clock the party was in full swing. Mac, Little Steven, and Big Al were eating peanut butter pretzels, trying to ignore the smell of grilled meat coming from the Morris's yard.

I'm starving, Mac, Big Al said. Come on. Let's go over. Just a few minutes.

Yeah, said Little Steven. We don't have to stay. We can grab a burger and come back.

Mac shook his head. They don't know you guys. Besides, it would be rude to go grab food and leave.

Rude? Big Al said. How would they even notice? There are tons of people over there. Besides, we're your guests. You can bring guests, can't you?

Mac drained his beer. I don't know.

Put it this way, Big Al said, I'm going. You can come if you want. He stood and made a show of tucking his shirt in. Don't want to be *rude*.

Okay, okay, Mac said, but thirty minutes max. He ran a hand over his chin. I got to shave, OK? Then we can go.

Jesus God in a bucket, Big Al said.

The grill was packed with dogs and burgers and there was a line of little kids waiting, so Mac grabbed a beer from the cooler and leaned against the Morris house assessing the scene. The family from India stood out; they had three nice-looking boys and the wife was easy to spot with the sari. There was a gaggle of little kids, hair so white-blonde it had no color. Boys, girls, all looked the same at that age, all elbows and knees. The adults he didn't recognize. New people, young mostly, who bought the lake houses Mac knew so well growing up and hired people to take them down to the studs and build them back up again. Mac loved the look of those naked planks and gutted insides; you could see how the buildings were put together. The big nails. Real wood planks. The structure looked honest, like it could be on a prairie, not in rural New York.

Neil jostled his shoulder. I'm surprised you came over, he said. I know you hate crowds.

Mac shrugged.

I don't know why he needs to set off so many fireworks, Neil said. It's ostentatious.

Everyone loves fireworks on the Fourth of July, Mac said grimly.

People with dogs hate them. Neil pointed toward the grill. Brought some friends, I see.

Yeah, we couldn't resist the smell.

How come your mom's not here?

She went to some women's retreat over near Ithaca.

Neil lowered his voice. I lost my job, you know.

I heard.

Who told you?

Guys at the gym, Mac said.

They probably thought it was a big joke, right? That I'm a joke.

People are idiots.

Neil caught a glimpse of his father staring at him from across the lawn. My parents have barely spoken to me since I got fired. My dad, mostly.

He's a dick, Mac said.

Nothing new there, Neil said.

Neil's dad was ex-navy. He went into war junky mode with Mac whenever Neil was around to hear, like sitting in a ship waiting for Japan to surrender was the same as walking ambush patrols along a 151-mile DMZ. My, son, he'd say, slapping Neil on the back. He's a lover, not a fighter, right Mac?

Fuck Mr. Morris and his gray-haired war.

Mac could see that Big Al and Little Steven were trying to look inconspicuous, but they weren't pulling it off. They were too damn big. Neil nudged Mac with his elbow. You better go over before something bad happens, he said.

Mr. Morris had noticed the crew from Mac's the second they arrived. Big guys, and no one he recognized. He'd have to keep an eye on that. He liked his new, rich neighbors and he didn't want anyone giving them a bad impression. Mrs. Morris watched Mac's friends warily too. They'd better not swear in front of the little kids, she thought. Or the Indians. She was hacking up a watermelon, one eye on the knife, and one on the guys waiting for burgers. Those two were familiar but she couldn't place them the way they were now, grown out of any little boy bodies she might have known from when Neil was young. She wanted them gone. Mac, too.

Mac got to the grill just as Big Al reached over a kid's head for a paper plate and lost his balance, knocking against the tiki torch, already lit for the night's activities. The torch tipped, caught the edge of the tablecloth and set it on fire. Little Steven grabbed oven mitts and smothered the flames, but the little kids were yelling *Fire! Fire!* and everyone at the party was looking, wondering if they had to do something. Mr. Morris thought, there's my cue.

Hey fellas, he said quietly, pulling Big Al and Little Steven aside, a hand firmly gripped on each man's biceps. How about you head back over to Mac's for a bit. We're happy to have you when it's a little less crowded. Make sense?

Big Al shook Morris off. Let go of me, asshole.

It's okay, Al, Mac said. We can come back later. He steered Big Al toward a break in the forsythia. Come on, Steven.

Little Steven reached into the cooler and took out six beers, piled them in his stretched-out T-shirt and followed Mac and Al. The glass bottles clinked with every step. At the hedge, he turned and gave Mr. Morris the finger. Mr. Morris pretended not to see. What he did see was his son Neil, standing against the house, grinning like a damn idiot.

Big Al sank into a beach chair. Here's a fun fact, Big Al said. Golden retrievers know when you're going to faint. Not all dogs can do it. Just Goldens. They bark like crazy.

Why do you suppose that is? Little Steven said, lowering himself gingerly into a chair. What purpose does it serve? I can see what advantage the human gets, but what about the dog? Do they get chosen more often for mates, like they're more sensitive? Or does it give them a head start, like something's wrong and they need to watch out for themselves? What does fainting even smell like?

Shut up Steven, Big Al said. It's just a fact. A fun fact.

You know what's not fun? Little Steven said. Being kicked out of a party. You ever been booted from that picnic before, Mac?

Mac slumped down in his chair, sipped his beer and closed his eyes. He was starting to feel the sweet unmooring that comes with enough alcohol. I don't think so.

So where does Morris get off?

He's a jerk, Mac said. He's always been like that.

Is Neil still as weird as he was in high school? Little Steven asked.

Do you think you two could shut up for a few minutes? Mac's thigh wouldn't stop jiggling and he couldn't keep his eyes off the shed, where he had a clear view of Mr. Morris stacking up the fireworks to bring down to the beach.

Anyway, Big Al continued, I think it's messed up that piece-of-shit Morris asked us to leave. You're their neighbor.

It's a disgrace, Little Steven agreed.

It's unpatriotic, that's what it is, Big Al said. I mean, you're a veteran for God's sake. It's the Fourth of July. You got that Bowie album, Mac? I think we need to play "Young Americans" real loud.

Try my old room.

It was the winter they were thirteen; Mac was home from Brode Academy for Christmas. Mac and Neil had discovered a construction pit that had filled with a few feet of water and frozen over. The ice was crap—it had warts and thick spots that slowed you down—but decent enough that the two of them spent an hour whacking a stone across the freeze and pretending they were the Buffalo Sabres. Neil was working up some real speed, rushing toward Mac with a fat stick raised over his head when he hit a leaf clump and went down hard, cracked a hole in the ice, and slid all the way under. For a long five seconds Neil was gone, a dark shape thrashing under the surface. Then Neil's head popped up, gasping. Mac grabbed his jacket. Take it easy, Neil, he said, trying to keep his voice calm. Go slow. Neil got a knee, then both legs on thicker ice and Mac held onto him until they could climb back out of the pit. Neil rose to his feet, white-faced. He wouldn't speak, wouldn't dump the water out of his boots. They slogged home in silence.

Why didn't you empty your boots, you idiot? Mr. Morris said when they got into Neil's kitchen.

Mac and Neil went their separate ways during the school year—they had different friends, different lives—but during the summers they'd find each other again. The summer after Mac's dad died, they discovered "Riders on the Storm" and would lie on the floor of Neil's bedroom, swallow a quarter tab of acid and listen to the song over and over. Sometimes they'd talk. Not about themselves, but about consciousness and death, and how time can bend, and how many realities can exist at once. Bullshit stuff. Sometimes Neil reached out and stroked Mac's hair and Mac didn't stop him. Then Mr. Morris would come home, and Neil's mom would call upstairs for Neil to come down for dinner and Mac would giggle like his gut would burst trying to keep a straight face as he walked past Neil's parents.

Summer before senior year Mrs. Morris discovered them lying with the top of their heads touching, sharing headphones blasting *Dark Side of the Moon.* She backed out of Neil's room quickly—Oh, excuse me. You boys were so quiet I didn't know you were here—and closed the door. She never said a word to Neil or Mac, but after that, Mac wasn't allowed upstairs. Instead, Neil and Mac snuck into the shed on Sunday afternoons. Neil brought his stereo and wired it up. Mac plugged in his lava lamp. They leaned a crowbar against the door and touched in the dark, the smell of warm lumber filling their heads, a kaleidoscope of colorful blobs floating around them.

One Sunday Mac and Neil found Mrs. Morris waiting for them in front of the shed with her arms crossed and a look on her face that made clear what she thought.

This would destroy your father if he ever found out, Neil, she said, furious. This stops right now. Understood? Right now.

Call it a reconnaissance mission, Mac, Big Al called out from the house. He was shuffling through Mac's albums. You're friends with them. You've got to go back and get us some burgers. I'm so hungry I got rubber chicken legs.

And watermelon, Little Steven added. Grab that too.

Mac looked through the hedge at the picnic. There were only a few teenagers hanging around the grill. He could make a surgical strike and be back in minutes.

Okay, but only me, Mac said. You guys stay here.

He cut through the forsythia, went straight to the grill, scooped up six burgers and six buns, piled them on a paper plate and jammed the mustard bottle in his back pocket. He held the back door open for the Indian lady with a dog in her purse, then snuck in and went straight to the kitchen. No one in sight; the watermelon sat on the counter. He could hear teenage girls laughing in the den, but all the other guests were on the beach waiting for the fireworks to start. Mac piled as many watermelon slices as he could on another paper plate and snuck out the back door of the house. The night was going gray to black. A sudden burst of bright light silhouetted the crabapple in the Morris's back yard. Mac's heart frog-kicked in his chest and he hunched his shoulders against the ear-splitting bang that followed.

Leaving so soon? The voice came from the yard. Neil, lying face down in the grass.

Mac steadied the watermelon and burgers and let his eyes adjust. You okay, Neil?

He flipped over. No. Everything's fucked up. My whole life. Who's going to hire me now? I'll lose my apartment. I can't move back in here with them. I'll die.

Watermelon juice was leaking down Mac's arm and sopping his T-shirt. The fizz of a chrysanthemum firework snaked into the sky.

Why does he have to do this every year? Neil said, shielding his eyes against the bright explosion of violet. Why do people even like fireworks?

The bang echoed. Mac's skin went clammy. He took a slow

breath in. Letters to the gods, he said. Like when people write messages on paper and burn them.

What people?

Korean people.

You sound like Big Al. Neil lifted himself to his elbows. Listen, Mac—

You know what I'd wish for? Mac interrupted, his voice suddenly loud. I'd wish the rest of the fireworks were duds. For starters. For a real quiet, without talking. With crickets in it.

Neil slumped back to the ground.

The whiz of a skyrocket shot through the night. Mac watched the streamer loft and fall in blue arcs. He held his breath; the silence afterward was unbearable. Mac shifted the plate to one arm and held tight to the porch railing, waited for the blast. Then it came, a bang so deafening it rattled the windows of Neil's house. The yellow of the backyard lights was making Mac nauseous. He took a few deep breaths. Everything that should have been still, tilted. Everything that should have been familiar, wasn't: where there should be shed, grass, picnic table, there was barbed wire, exploded rice paddy, holes. He instinctively scanned the yard, alert for footprints in the sand, a break in the fence.

There was a quick succession of pops, and a band of pain tightened around Mac's head. His nostrils felt swollen like he couldn't get enough air in, and when he squeezed his eyes shut, shots of light crossed his eyelids. He opened them. His arm multiplied when he lifted it, twelve arms. The burgers and watermelon slid off their plates into the dirt. Mac covered his ears with his hands.

Okay, okay, Neil said, jumping up. I'm getting you somewhere quiet. Let's go inside.

No, Mac hissed. There are kids there. I don't want to see anyone.

This way then, Neil said. He led Mac across the yard to the shed. A series of chrysanthemums rose in smoky trails, paused, and exploded in the shape of blooms, all red and blue. Neil shouldered open the shed door, sat Mac down on the tool bench, and nudged the door closed. Better?

The next rocket was muffled.

Mac nodded. The warmth and closeness of the shed calmed him. The shelves of amber lanterns and cobalt flasks, the smell of pine planks after a long July day, the ghosts of their young selves, all created a rush of love in him. Mac had always measured kindnesses against Neil's. His memories—this shed, this boy—battled with what he now knew about bodies. How they go together, how they're torn apart.

There was another skyrocket's muffled blast, and afterward, cheering. Light from the next explosion flashed across the walls of the shed. Neil squatted and took Mac's hands in his. His father's fireworks would be another success, thought Neil. Seemed so simple, what makes you happy. "Come," he said.

Somewhere far away, a dog wouldn't stop barking.

Big Al and Little Steven sat in Mac's beach chairs, eyes closed, nodding their heads to their own thoughts and the beat of the stereo. Big Al had found the Bowie record and turned the speakers to blast "Young Americans" into the Morris's yard.

I'm seriously starving, Little Steven said. I may faint from hunger.

Big Al thought Little Steven did look pale. Morris probably ran out of food, he said, disgusted. Or Mac would be back with our burgers by now.

Morris is heinous.

Majorly heinous.

He took Mac's shed.

Without asking.

And put all his crap in there.

Worthless crap.

Big Al put down his beer. It's the Fourth of July, right?

Yeah.

And on the Fourth of July it's traditional to have a bonfire, right?

Traditional *and* patriotic.

And everybody's down at the lake except us, right?

That's right.

Big Al lifted himself out of his chair. We're in agreement?

We are.

Then turn up the music.

Little Steven pumped the stereo so that he could feel the bass in his chest. Big Al soaked the back and sides of the shed with lighter fluid. He stood back, lit a match, tossed it and hollered. Up to the gods, assholes!

The fire caught so quickly he had to run to keep from going up with it. In a second the ground was hot and grasshoppers flew wild toward the sky. Little Steven and Big Al pressed themselves against Mac's house and listened in awe to the rushing sound of fire inhaling and exhaling, the sound of a dark angel consuming everything, changing everything. It was loud, louder than Bowie, louder than the explosion of fireworks over the lake, raging, terrible.

The shed's roof buckled, and flames threw up sparks and kicked the knees out of the support boards until the whole wall collapsed like a mother watching her only son lowered into a grave. A cinder flew up and landed on a crisp, draught-starved leaf on the crabapple tree. It lit, burned around the edges, shriveled, and fell the ground at their feet.

By the time everyone got there, the heat radiated ten feet out.

Goddammit, Mr. Morris said, distraught. Dammit to hell. He shook his head in fury. Explosions popped like gunfire as glass shattered and shot cobalt shards onto the lawn. His wife stood next to him, anxiously rubbing his arm. Other guests watched, red-skulled in the light of the flames. A shadow passed over her face.

Where's Neil? Mrs. Morris asked. The light from the fire spread down the side of her face as she turned to search the yard. Where's Neil? she said, louder, panicking. The shed roof collapsed. Neil! she screamed. Mr. Morris lunged forward in time to catch his wife around the waist and pin her to his chest. She strained against his arms, screaming her son's name, over and over. Her voice was lost in the hiss of fire, sound of sirens in the distance.

But Neil and Mac were blind to the embers rising in the dark, deaf to the sirens and shouting from below. They were safe at the old sugar shack, their bodies pressed close—skin against skin, hearts, thighs, lips—two boys skating together as one in the sweetness of a pine forest high above the lake, so pristine and still, like perfect ice.

4

LAKE SONG

This is the truth about a small town: for good or for ill, there is a We. What one sees, another hears; what one hears, another holds. The wind that silvers the leaves of the birch also lifts pillowcases on the line, ripples the goldenrod, kisses the back of the neck of a town worker pouring hot tar into cracks in the asphalt. We move on the same stage, lift and balance each other, cry tears down each other's cheeks, sing the same song of water: waves, rocks, rainbow trout jumping at mayflies. We ride in boats at night, lighting matches to find each other in the dark. We. We.

The Room at the End of the Hall

Fourth of July, Frances Price thought. Independence Day. For-
tuitous date or a mean joke, she wondered. She got out of
Palmetto's taxi at the cemetery gate. It was late afternoon, sun
high in the sky, hot. Wait here, would you, Tony? she asked.

Sure thing, Ms. P.

As she walked, Frances sang the song her mother had sung
whenever they passed a graveyard:

The stones stone deaf, the lonely stones,
The cold wet stones, the lichen stones,
The stones in rain, the stones in snow,
The stones in rows, the secret stones,
The silent stones, our precious ones.

There were Sam and Dorie Fish on each side of their little
Eli, together at last. Evelyn Dunn lay somewhere near the obe-
lisk marked with the family name in eighteen-inch-high serif,
and Mitchell Epps's wife, Carol, in the Epps crypt with all the
rest of them, too young. The oldest stones belonged to the
Staunches: Clara and Joseph and their poor Mavis, drowned
in Okisee when she was only twenty-six. Frances stood in front
of the cemetery's newest grave, but her voice was so lodged in
her throat that she couldn't say *goodbye, Helen* although that
is what she'd come to do. I'll miss our visits, she wanted to say,

but I've got to go where the living are. The truth was—and she knew Helen knew it—that Frances didn't want to live in a place where the dead could appear at any moment and catch you up. Grief was a monster.

Frances composed her face and headed back to the cab. Sorry, Tony, my shoes are muddy. He shrugged.

They hadn't gone but a mile when Frances spied old Mitchell Epps walking along the side of the road in a gray, three-piece Sunday suit, an apricot ascot the only pop of color. His walk was the unmistakable bowlegged walk of a farmer, but somehow gentlemanly, with his hands clasped behind his back. Frances knew that Mitchell's mind had wandered with age, and as they got closer, she could see that he looked confused. Stop, she told Tony. Frances got out of the cab.

What are you up to, Mitchell? she asked, holding onto his elbow and walking alongside him. His face was red with the heat, and he dabbed at his forehead with a neatly folded handkerchief.

I'm not sure, Mitchell said. I think I'm a bit lost.

Can I help? Frances asked.

Milk, Mitchell said brightly. We need milk back at the house.

Where were you going to get that up here?

Mitchell looked down at his feet and laughed. I don't know, he said. Maybe I was just out for a walk.

You've got to be more careful, Mitchell. The road is so broken up around here; you could fall.

Walking is falling, Frances. Every single step, you've got to catch yourself. He stopped suddenly and cocked his head. Oh, oh! Listen, Frances! Do you hear that? The lake is singing! Isn't it glorious?

Frances strained to listen.

Stand right here. He placed Frances in front of him. A wind

lifted the canopy of leaves and Frances heard it: the Episcopal church choir practicing in the vestry far below them. Okisee Lake carried sound in the most unexpected ways.

Mitchell swayed to the music, his eyes closed. Then he opened them and smiled at her. I'm not as looney as you think, Frances Price.

Let me give you a ride home, Mitchell. You'll get heat stroke walking up here; you're overdressed. Frances guided Mitchell to the cab's back seat. She got in next to him.

The smell of mulberries was so strong they could taste them on their tongues. They rode along the back roads toward Mitchell's farmhouse until they came up behind a slow-moving Ford pickup with a gaggle of young kids in the truck bed shooting spitballs at each other through straws. One little girl wore a crown and carried a paper torch.

Is the Fourth of July parade today? Mitchell asked. Something nipped at his heart; he couldn't place the memory.

It is, Frances said, smiling and waving at the children.

The pickup driver waved for them to pass the truck.

You were up at the cemetery, Frances?

Yes. Saying goodbye, I suppose. I'm leaving Kinder Falls, moving to Rochester. She looked at Mitchell's profile. A face worn out and surrendering to gravity, ears too large for his face now.

Mitchell smiled at her. So, you're one of those, he said.

One of what?

One of the leaving birds, he said. Mitchell leaned his head against the back of the seat and sighed. I'm a staying bird, although I've often wished it weren't so. So many wonderful people are leaving birds.

Frances touched Mitchell's knee. What do you hear from your Caroline?

Nothing yet. It'll take her a bit to get settled in Chicago, I imagine.

How old is she now?

Twenty-something.

Frances nodded. The selfish years.

Mitchell suddenly sat up in the seat. Will she figure it out, Frances? Or those little ones we passed in the wagon? Will they figure it out?

Figure what out, Mitchell?

What they're meant to do. How to fix the things we didn't.

Frances patted Mitchell's knee. Caroline will be fine.

I hate thinking of her all alone.

We all start alone, don't we, Mitchell?

And finish, too.

Don't be bleak, Mitchell. Look down at the lake. It's absolutely beautiful right now.

Mitchell turned to look out the taxi's window. Do you think there's a difference between people who live near water and people who don't?

Maybe, Frances said. Probably.

It's queer, isn't it, Mitchell said, this older, old age. I feel like I'm walking down a long hallway closing doors behind me, and when I get to the end there's only a bed in a small room and it's time to turn in. Funny phrase, isn't it? Turn in. Like you bend yourself into smaller and smaller selves until you'd fit in a pocket. I feel like I've done that most of my life, folded myself smaller.

Yes, Frances thought. These were the disappearing years for sure. Time to turn in.

Mitchell put out his hand, palm up, and Frances placed hers in it.

I think it will come like a jack-in-the-box, Mitchell said.

Dying. You expect it of course, but it still makes you jump. And suddenly there's no time left to finish things, only minutes, seconds. You have to leave it all like an untied shoelace for the ones who come up after you.

Frances gazed out the car window. Caroline will be fine, Mitchell. You did good with her.

Adria had rented a van to haul all of Frances's things from the Kinder Falls house to her new apartment in Rochester. When they were loaded inside, she helped Frances into the passenger seat and buckled her in. It was getting late.

For god's sake, Adria, Frances said, frowning at the belt. I'm not going to run away.

I hate driving after dark, Adria said. I can't see all that well.

Jesus, Frances said, and pulled the belt tighter.

The van drove slowly down Water Street, then, when it hit the outskirts of Kinder Falls, Adria turned onto the two-lane and the town disappeared behind them. Lights from the lake flashed between trees until that too was gone. The van climbed up a steep hill. Frances looked at the neatly planted vineyards stretching out on either side of the road. Grapes, corn, maple trees; this part of the world was sweet with sugar, she thought. She turned for one last look, and a series of bright red fireworks exploded in the sky illuminating everything: trees, fence, power lines, sumac, chicory, timothy grass, road. She took it all in, tried to burn it into her memory, bring it with her into that little room at the end of the hall.

Look! Adria said, pointing to the field on her right. It was an orphaned well site, now re-Edening itself with saplings. Do you see them?

Frances could barely make out the deer at the edge of the field: dark shapes against the trees. At least two dozen, even more. Noses down, nibbling grass. She was entranced. Slow down, Adria, she said. Adria stopped the van. Frances rolled down her window stuck her arm out and waved. Goodbye, stunning, glorious things! she called. They raised their heads all at the same time, sniffed the air, and bounded quickly into the woods, white tails flicking, vanishing away from this world into theirs.

The Final Girl

1994

Marlena

This is the land in winter, when snow covers the fields like cream, going from white to a weak blue to rose to gold as the sun sets. At dark, snowmelt freezes in the ruts of the dirt roads and the birds go black against tree branches. It is a brittle time. Ice has formed under the docks and along the edges of the creeks around Okisee. This is a kind of cold that the people of west central New York know deeply: How it blows across the lake with nothing to stop it. How it enters the brick of the chimney and stays, how it flattens itself against glass and frosts the insides of windows. Every February the people of Kinder Falls look longingly at their photos of a Florida vacation taken before their children were born and imagine they'll live there someday, when they finish their working lives. But they don't. They stuff rags around the loose panes and tuck towels under the front and back doors and carry on, going to the supermarket, to the town hall and post office, to the sale at Sears, to the fancy restaurant that puts blue cheese crumbles on their salads, and to the Holiday Inn function room to watch the child in town who plays chess compete in an adult competition where the prize is a free haircut.

But with March comes promise. The light is lengthening and the green that lies underground is unwinding itself.

It was the sunlight in March—a sap-starting, snow-washed, ice-melting light—that made Marlena pack her ten-month-old baby into the car seat and drive 160 miles from Scranton to Kinder Falls. She needed to move, to drive, to go, and this was the place she'd known as a girl, the place she came back to even through college, even after she got married, and even after Aunt Lucy moved away and her sons sold the house, because it was a beautiful, begin-again place. And now here she was, checking into a Red Roof Inn to show it all to June, beautiful baby June, happy June. And there was Kathy behind the counter, like always.

Well, look what the cat dragged in.

Hey, Kathy. How's your mom?

Cranky as ever. What are you doing back here in the winter?

It's technically spring, right? Weekend getaway. Have you got a room you can give me for a few days? Not facing the parking lot if you have it. Marlena sat June on the counter. When did they get a Walmart over in Dryden?

Three years ago, maybe? Put the Dollar General pretty much out of business. Look at this gorgeous baby. What's her name?

June.

And what brings you here in mud season? You nuts?

Roger is getting remarried, and I told him he could use my apartment for the in-laws.

Oh? I didn't know you two had split.

Over two years now.

Sorry.

Don't be. Everyone was pretty much relieved when it happened.

Kathy wiggled June's toes. But . . . you have a baby?

A happy accident.

Who's the dad?

Navy guy.

In Scranton?

Marlena laughed. His parents live there. He was home on leave.

Kathy raised her eyebrows.

No, he's not in the picture.

Single again, Marlena had been liberal with her body, careless, with her navy man. She never dreamed she'd get pregnant at forty-two, but sperm found egg and grew, two cells, twenty-four, and Marlena couldn't decide what to do. Hands, lungs, eyes, and still Marlena stalled. Bones, hair, toenails, ears, June.

She'd known the man only a few weeks, had a picture and a matchbook from the Cantina Bar where they'd met. But she was coming to know him more intimately in the parts of June that weren't her. A single dimple in the cheek, length of thigh, June's eyes, not violet like Marlena's, but a warm brown. He'd left for Bahrain before she knew she was pregnant, and she couldn't decide whether to tell him, or how, or when. Now that June was here, she couldn't imagine anyone else in their little family. She knew it was selfish, but aren't all parents selfish in some way? Roger had never wanted kids, a different kind of selfishness.

Kathy walked her fingers up the baby's legs and tickled her chin. I can do $120 for a long weekend. Friends and family discount. Though a real friend would keep in touch.

You're the best, Kathy.

I know. Kathy glanced out the hotel's front window and frowned. Crap. Sharon Epps.

Really? Marlena watched a woman climb heavily out of a Bronco. I thought all the Epps were gone.

All but her, Kathy said. You remember her father—sweet,

old Mitchell Epps? He died just last month. Sharon lives alone now in that big farmhouse near old drill pad.

That's sad.

Which? Mitchell, Sharon, or the pad?

All of them, I guess. Marlena picked up June and settled her on a hip. I remember thinking the pumpjack looked like a giraffe when I first saw it. I thought it was beautiful. I was probably fourteen.

Kathy shook her head. Yeah, well no.

The door to the lobby jingled as it opened. Sharon Epps came halfway in and swung the door back and forth to set the bells jingling. Ho ho ho! Hey, fat Kathy. Colder than a witch's tit, right? She shut the door behind her and squinted at Marlena. I've seen you before, haven't I?

Marlena smiled weakly at the woman staring at her. A large, flat face. Tufts of greying hair flew out at her temples, the rest drawn back in a low ponytail. Her T-shirt said It's Wine O' Clock! and the button on her pants pressed deep into her flab.

I've got a couple Wall Street burnouts who think they want to start a winery coming Saturday to take a look at my land, Sharon said to Kathy. You got a room this weekend? They're morons, but I'll take their money.

You selling it all? Kathy asked.

If I can. Selling it and getting outta Dodge.

Where to?

Not sure. Someplace without snow, ice, or mud.

Marlena jiggled the baby, who had started to fidget. Sharon wheeled around.

A baby girl! she said. Her voice swung into a high register. Oh, hello sweetheart, you precious thing.

Sharon wiggled June's foot. Such a cutie pie. Hello little darling. What's your name?

This is June, Marlena said.

Hello June, Sharon cooed. Aren't you perfect. Can I hold her? Just for a minute.

No, sorry, I was about to feed her, she's hungry.

Kathy passed a key card to Marlena. You can have 103.

Come on, Sharon said. I'm great with little babies. Anyone will tell you that.

Sorry. Marlena scooted around Sharon, hitched June up on her hip, and slung her bag over her shoulder. The door jingled.

Ho ho ho! Sharon yodeled. She turned to Kathy. Well, she's a real bitch, isn't she?

Kathy stared past Sharon at the parking lot. A squirrel arced across the pavement.

Now that I think of it, I recognize her. It's that jet black hair. It used to be long—down to her ass. She's a Staunch, right? Came in the summers and stayed with Lucy? She was here that week the kid died at Schuyler's Creek.

I don't remember, Kathy said. She drummed her fingers on the counter.

So, what room can you give me for my people?

Marlena had packed impulsively, didn't quite think it through, all the things you'd need for a long weekend with a baby: more diapers, lotion, a teething ring. She'd have to get to a store before everything closed. Her best friend Ruth said it was mom brain; she'd read it had to do with hormones.

Marlena's room phone rang. Call for you on 42, Kathy said. It's Roger.

Marlena steeled herself and picked up the receiver.

We can't find the blue thing, Roger said.

She heard Vicki, Roger's bride-to-be, in the background.

The sapphire, Vicki whined. It was in a Tiffany box. I put it on the TV. Remember, Marlena? You said it was lovely.

Yeah, Roger said. She can't find the something blue that she needs for the wedding.

I remember seeing it, Marlena said. But no, I don't know where it went. Did you look behind the couch?

Yes, we looked behind the couch, Roger said. We've looked everywhere. What's with the fish, Marlena?

June likes to watch them.

Okay. Well, um. Thanks anyway.

That Roger had asked her to house her ex-in-laws for his wedding was so presumptuous that Marlena had been stunned into silence, and now there they were—her one-time sister-in-law, her one-time mother-in-law—sleeping in her bed and making coffee in her kitchen, getting ready to celebrate Roger and the so-called love of his life, Vicki. Even the name was like a pinch. She reached over to her bag and pulled out the Tiffany box, pried open the lid, and admired the sapphire ring. She slipped it on her finger. Marlena smiled to herself. Vicki was welcome to this mother-in-law, she thought. The woman had referred to Marlena as "the renter" when she'd moved in with Roger. Marlena dialed Ruth's number and left a message. She'd forgotten to ask Ruth to feed the fish, and she wasn't going to ask her ex-in-laws to do it.

The hotel's brown shag rug and gold-and-maroon striped drapes were faded. The sink had a brown stain in the shape of a kidney and the bedspread was damp. Marlena wished she'd brought more clothes and toys. She'd always thought of herself as a free spirit, expansive and adventurous, but sometimes she wondered if she was simply a scatterbrained fool.

June was whimpering. Marlena lifted the baby to her breast and settled into a chair to watch the trees outside her window, dark like black velvet. She ran her finger across the tiny pimples that dotted each of June's cheeks. Her perfect ears, nearly invisible brows, tiny nails. After, Marlena buckled a sleepy June into her car seat and drove a mile to the Quick Mart.

The first flakes looked like a mistake: princess-light, cartoon-lovely. She admired them, pointed them out to June. The store was nearly empty, and the cashier stared into the middle distance, arms folded, as Marlena unpacked her cart with one hand, June clutched in the other.

Sorry, I'm a little slow.

The girl stared out the plate glass window and pretended she hadn't heard. The snow was coming thicker now. In her summers here, Marlena remembered how quickly the weather could turn, how fast and hard the rain came in, like a wall, and left. You could watch it travel the lake: first a silent grayness far away, then a rush of cold and an exhilarating darkness, then the rain. Big droplets, like frogs falling from the sky. Then, almost as fast as it came it vanished, and the sun painted wet surfaces so that the whole beach sparkled. You could watch the gray retreat, like it had all been a joke.

Marlena protected June with her coat until they reached the car. The sky was a cypher: dark, but moving, swirling. Was the storm coming or going? She couldn't see the lake from here.

A bearded man in a slicker loaded bags of snow melt into his truck.

How bad's it supposed to be? Marlena called to him.

Four inches? Maybe more, he said. But the wind, I guess. Strong wind.

Marlena got June in her car seat and then buckled herself in. She'd made it in the nick of time. The Quick Mart lights went dark, and the cashier dashed through the parking lot, got into the man's Ford, and the truck pulled away. Marlena smiled at June in the rearview mirror. It's okay, sweetie, she said. We'll be back at the hotel soon. She turned the key. Nothing. She pumped the gas pedal. Start, she prayed, panic rising in her chest. Nothing. She stomped on the pedal, a sweat breaking out on her lip. The engine turned over, yes! then stalled. She pumped again. Turned the key. Nothing. Marlena's stomach tightened. She tried again. Nothing. Engine's probably flooded, she thought. I'll give it a few minutes. She looked around at June, who stared back with big, worried eyes. It's okay, Junie, she crooned, everything's all right. Want your binky? Marlena rifled through her purse. Diapers, Kleenex, lip balm, golf pencil, but no pacifier. Damn. She tried the ignition again. Not a flicker. She unbuckled her seatbelt. It was a mile to the hotel; she could walk it in twenty minutes. She'd leave the groceries and come back in the morning.

June was in a fleece onesie, a hat, and a sweater; Marlena swore at herself for not putting the baby in a snowsuit. She zipped June inside her down coat, grabbed her bag and walked. Snow thickened the air, needle sharp. The wind picked up huge handfuls and whipped the flakes in her face. She kept to the side of the road, head down, singing to June: you are my sunshine, my only sunshine. Marlena's eyes watered and her feet were wet and going numb, not good. She thought she'd been walking about ten minutes when a light appeared in the distance. A car! She waved wildly. It slowed, pulled over, stopped. A Bronco. The driver's window opened.

I remember your hair. You had long, black hair, down to your ass.

Sharon had a hood pulled tight around her face. Marlena saw only darkness of eyes and lips, tight and thin. She felt a hitch in her gut and hugged June closer into her chest.

Get in, for God's sake.

Marlena hesitated.

Sharon leaned over and opened the passenger door. You insane?

Marlena and June slid in.

Thank you, Marlena said. My car wouldn't start.

It's your battery.

No, I had a new battery put in a few months back.

I know cars, Sharon snapped. It's your battery. She looked over at June's little face peeking out of Marlena's coat. Hey, sweet thing. June made a quiet, whining sound. Oh, don't you make sad noises, now, cutie pie. Sharon reached into Marlena's coat and took June's finger. We're friends, okay?

Marlena slid toward the door, away from Sharon. I really appreciate your giving us a ride, she said. The windshield had steamed up and she was sweating in the car's heat. June fidgeted and kicked until Marlena unzipped her coat and sat the baby on her lap. On the dash, a plastic hula girl swung her hips.

No problem, Sharon said, her eyes locked on June.

The snow was already a white veil across the windshield.

We really need to get to the Red Roof, Sharon. June's not dressed for this.

Sharon tugged on June's toes. She doesn't feel cold to me. She put her face close to the baby's. June's eyes widened. I could eat your fat little cheeks, she said. I could eat you with a spoon, yes I could. Such a sweet girl, precious angel. Sharon glanced up at Marlena. You want to get going, do you?

Yes, if we could, please.

Then let me hold her. Just for a second.

June sneezed, then laughed at herself.

See, Sharon said, even the baby thinks it's a good idea. Let me hold her. Then we can go.

A plow's headlights hit Sharon's face and it lit up. Marlena felt the same hitch in her gut. She had the sense of being with a teenager, not a grown woman, and it was such a strong feeling that she checked Sharon's face again. There were gray spikes in her eyebrows, a sag under her chin, dark patches in the hollows of her cheeks. Still, the way she moved was like a teenager—mean, impulsive. Marlena found her voice. I'd rather you didn't.

Jesus Christ. I'm not going to hurt a baby. Let me hold her, then we'll go. No skin off your nose. Or do you want to sit here all night and argue about it?

Marlena loosened her grip on June.

Sharon smiled and lifted June gingerly. She held the baby on her lap like she was holding a much larger child; too loose. Marlena reached out a hand to steady June. Sharon pushed her hand away. Hey, sweetie-pie, she sang. You are too delicious. I'm going to eat you up, eat you up from head to toesies, I am. Sharon nibbled on June's shoulder and June giggled. Yum, yum.

We really need to go, Sharon.

No, you don't.

The baby's hungry, Marlena said.

No, she's not.

Sharon, please.

A minute passed. Two. The three of them filled the car with their breath and heat. Marlena felt sweat trickle down her back. She felt nauseous. She needed to be back at the hotel, away from Sharon, away from the snow, away from whatever this was. Sharon began to sing.

I peeked in to say goodnight, but my baby had flown away,
Flown away across the lake, bright red ribbons in her hair.

I peeked in to say goodnight, but my daddy had flown away,
Gone to live in Forest Gate, gone to live with angels there.

Sharon's voice was low and tuneless. Her eyes were closed, like she'd forgotten the snow, the Bronco, Marlena.

Sharon, Marlena said quietly. Kathy told me about your dad. I'm so sorry. I remember he used to drive all us kids in his truck in the Fourth of July parades. I thought he was the kindest man I'd ever known. I can't imagine how much you miss him.

Sharon's face contorted into grimace; she squeezed her eyes shut and hugged June closer.

I'll take the baby back now, Marlena said. She moved closer to Sharon and reached for June, but Sharon twisted away.

Sharon's voice was whispery. Not yet. I need another minute. Just one more minute. She rested her cheek on June's head and looked at Marlena. Please?

Give her to me, Sharon.

No.

Let her go, Sharon.

No.

Marlena reached for June, but Sharon clutched the baby tighter, too tight, and June gave a wail, then another, louder, and another, until the red-faced baby made an awful, choking sound and Sharon yelled *sorry, sorry, sorry,* and handed June to Marlena, who wrenched open the door of the Bronco, jumped out, and started walking.

The snow came at her in mean swirls, but Marlena put one foot in front of the other, hugging the hysterical baby inside her coat. It's okay, June, she said, it's okay now, breathe, sweetie, hush-a-bye, sweet Junie. We'll be back at the motel very, very soon. Rock-a-bye baby. It's alright now, it's alright, hush little baby. She could see only a few yards in front of her but felt the road under her sneakers. The world was loud with wind. A faint light behind her cast a shadow on the snow. The Bronco's headlights.

Sharon shouted out the window. I'll give you a ride to the Red Roof, I promise. Get in the car, for God's sake. You'll freeze out here. Don't be an idiot! She pulled closer to Marlena and laid on the horn.

Marlena took off into the trees. Her purse caught on a low branch and wrenched her shoulder. She yanked it free, ran faster, her heart banging, the baby's wails escalating. She heard Sharon yell, but wind swallowed the words. Marlena kept moving, tripping and sliding over roots and wet stones hidden under the snow. She stepped hard on something sharp, broken glass? that cut through her sneaker. She ran until she couldn't see ahead or behind her—the snow was a staticky blur in all directions—and only then did she stop. June, startled by the stillness and cold, went quiet. Marlena held her breath and listened; she could no longer hear Sharon. Her shoes were soaked and frozen, her fingers numb, and her hair dripped with snow. Freak snowstorm in March. Freak mother with baby. No clothes, no food. She swayed side to side rocking June, listening to the woods, waiting for the crack of the branch that would fall on them, the growl of coyote, the click of a rifle, Sharon. Her shoe was split open, the bottom of her foot sticky. Blood is not red. Blood is black against the snow.

A lump of freeze slid off a pine branch and thudded onto the ground, making her jump; was something moving through the trees? Marlena crouched down and prayed that June wouldn't cry. There, only ten feet away she saw a wizened, white-haired man. The snow circled, then settled. No, not a man; it was a buck, snow frosting his thick gray coat, half molted. Head up, smelling, antlers gone. Scraggly, hungry, nosing for new grass budding under the snow, his want-belly distended from a long, scarce winter. June whined. The buck leapt away, white tail flashing. Bleached leaves hung like dead bats on the trees.

Animals were warnings, auguries, omens, Marlena thought. This was good. She limped along, trying to follow the buck, but the animal left no footprints. Dampness clogged her lungs. She struggled to breathe in, out. Panic rose up and tightened her throat. She swallowed, concentrated. She'd been in these woods as a kid. She knew them. She could do this; she could find her way out. Around her, white pine. Pine resin seals, Aunt Lucy used to say, would staunch the blood from a wound.

You don't have to do this alone, Ruth told her when Marlena was eight months pregnant, and huge. They'd been wandering around Walmart looking for things a baby might need. Ruth handed her a pair of nail clippers so small they couldn't possibly be of use. There's a guy out there who could be good for both of you, she said.

I barely know him.

You liked him enough to sleep with him.

He's probably happier not knowing. He's on a ship on the other side of the world; how could he be the kind of man who wants a family?

How do you know he doesn't?

It's easier this way. It's my decision.

It's not fair to him. What's this for? Ruth had picked up a white noise machine.

So babies can sleep. It has the same sounds they hear in your stomach.

Seriously?

I don't know.

You should tell him.

And then what? Fight with him for her?

Marlena's previous loves—a few boyfriends, Roger—felt slight, untethered, as if they could drift away in a heartbeat, and they did. Her love for June was earth-bound, it was body, the very force that kept her feet on the ground.

Why assume the worst? Ruth asked.

Why assume otherwise?

What did Ruth know, Marlena thought. Ruth had never been married. She hadn't woken up on a Sunday morning to hear her husband confessing he was in love with a Vicki. Ruth had no idea how love disappoints. How it breaks the ground beneath you. How small you can become.

You have no idea, Ruth.

I know that you don't have to do this alone. At least let me come to the hospital when she's born. It shouldn't be you in there all by yourself, with only nurses.

Marlena had said yes. Ruth had come with her, and Ruth had sat with her through labor, but then went pale and wouldn't go into the birthing room.

Marlena had been alone, after all.

A sliver of a moon emerged and lit three wooden posts leaning into the earth. Marlena knew this place! As a girl, she'd found bottles from an old sugar shack here. As a girl she'd built fires here, played with boys here. Here is where her Aunt Lucy would come for the ramps that grew in the sweet soil of the maple trees, where she taught Marlena about plants. Marlena followed the drifts, walking and singing to June—another five minutes, another ten—sure she would find more familiar landmarks. There should be a hedge of yew and a rock that looked like a frog. But the snow flattened the landscape and she recognized nothing. A movement caught her eye: the buck, ahead in the distance. And in that direction, a solidness. She squinted. Marlena's spirits leapt. A house? She sprinted toward it, startling the buck, who bolted. Yes, a house! Stone walls. Broken shutters. One door with a rusted padlock. She picked up a rock and banged it against the metal, three, five, ten times. June screamed and screamed. It broke. Marlena was so grateful she laughed with delight. They entered. June took in the cold, dark, room and wailed.

Marlena pushed a broom handle through the latch to secure the door. She found a musty sleeping bag under a bed and wrapped the baby and herself in it. She swayed, cradling June against her shoulder. The house was quiet. There were only dead, boneless things in it: a hornet's nest that had papered itself to a beam, its ancient flaking skin torn open years before. Beside the bed, an abandoned mouse nest of chewed newspaper, spider silk, and wood shavings. Marlena relaxed in the comfort of wooden beam, of shelf, of chair. She fed June, who was ravenous. The smell of damp stone filled her nostrils.

The exhausted baby fell asleep. Marlena put her in a new diaper and swaddled June in her coat. The house was freezing. There was a log pile and old newspaper stacked next to the fireplace, so she opened the flue, arranged logs on the grate, crumpled sheets of newspaper and tucked them around the wood. She felt around the mantel and found a metal tin filled with matches. Work, work, work, she prayed. They did. When the fire got going, she peeled off her sock. A big gash bisected the ball of her foot; it was still bleeding and the skin around it rippled like waterlogged seaweed. She ripped a piece of her T-shirt with her teeth and wound it around her foot to stop the blood.

Marlena tried to stay awake. She sat by the fire with June and talked to her about their family and how their people were farmers, then rail workers, then salesmen of gloves and hats, then teachers, then phone company workers, car mechanics, and paralegals, as she was. She sounded out their names, as if

June's history could protect her: Mavis, Edith, Paula, several Johns, and of course June, a grandmother Marlena had loved. As she drifted, people flickered in the corners of the room, kind people, their hands open, offering cake, singing without words in a chorus like spring leaves ruffling. There was a blur of colors—bright greens and sapphire—of women in Queen Anne's lace-print dresses and movie star sunglasses and the bitter smell of gin. Gin like Juniper. Juniper like pine resin. Resin like canoes. A distant cousin who drowned in Okisee. A boy and a waterfall. A twin sister's face pressed flat against her own in her mother's womb. The dead, who float through mirrors and leave you. The living, who float through rooms and leave you. What do you want most? the navy man had asked her after their first night together. As if there was a thing. Snow in a streetlight. Grandmother's ice cubes in a glass. A hundred days like this. Marlena felt held in the time between breathing in and breathing out, where air is not necessary, or body. The corners of the stone house erupted in colors. Thank you, house, Marlena said without sound, sending her words through the air like paper lanterns.

When she woke, planks of sun lay down on the floorboards and bent up the walls. She felt newly hopeful, teenage-giddy. She'd wanted things so desperately as a girl: I want to live in a beautiful house, she'd told a boy once; I want to be famous. There was time yet, Marlena laughed to herself, and there are still miracles. There was June.

Marlena slipped out of the sleeping bag and lit another fire to warm them. She changed June's diaper and drew the baby to her breast. Marlena was starving. She rummaged in her purse and found two packages of peanut butter crackers. Another miracle! She cradled June with one arm and tore the wrappers with her teeth and devoured them. June sucked hungrily, then eyed her mother impishly and bit, a delighted look on her face.

Okay, then, Marlena said, you're done here. She tugged on her coat and shoes, picked up the baby, removed the broom handle and went outside. The bright sun made everything sparkle, as if the night's terror had never happened. Trees dripped snow-melt that made water prints in the drifts. Marlena scooped a handful of pristine snow and let it melt in her mouth.

Kathy was probably arriving at the hotel, wondering where Marlena could have gone so early in the morning. Someone might call the sheriff about the car abandoned in the Quick Mart lot. How about that snow, everyone would say. Came in fast, gone fast. And Sharon, that storm of a woman, she didn't frighten Marlena at all in the light of day.

Marlena kissed June and looked back at the stone house, another miracle. The name "Tuttle" was carved in lovely letters above the house's door. Whoever you are, Tuttle, she thought, we Staunch women thank you.

Glints of Okisee shone through the trees. The water was brilliant, as if the lake had inhaled the sun and then breathed it out in blinding bursts. Dead leaves clung to the old growth trees that dotted the hillside. Marlena remembered Aunt Lucy's word for it. Marcescent. Leaves that hang on until new growth pushes them out. Like people do. Like her. It wasn't that far she'd come, and yet it seemed Marlena had been jettisoned into another life. She'd tell her navy guy about June. If it worked out with him, great. If it didn't, she knew she could manage alone. But really, she hoped it would.

Squirrels on a branch sent down a shower of powder. She walked through the curtain of snow into a clearing where she had a better view of the water. The baby pointed: that tree, that rock, that airplane rumbling high above. She turned June toward the lake. Look, June. See how bright the water is? I used to come here as a girl, and you will too. You will learn to swim, like I did, and you will fish, and canoe, and build forts from pine branches like I did. A red-tailed hawk circled high above them, hungry, merciless. A quick wind rose and the lake thumbed page after page after page onto the shore.

June pointed. Her face was serious, her eyes focused on something far away. What is it, June? A duck? A chipmunk? Marlena looked in the direction of the baby's gaze; the lake was empty but for a solitary canoe, stilled, no wake. June stretched her tiny arms out as if reaching for it. You're not going anywhere, Marlena said, and she wished it was true, that she could keep June here, with her, in this moment, but June wriggled, trying to squirm out of Marlena's arms, as she would always, as children do. Marlena shifted June to get a better grip, and they walked toward the lake, toward the road and its happy morning traffic, two figures growing smaller and smaller until they disappeared in the glare of the sun.

Lake Layers

Mavis

What falls to the bottom is like snow, but not: wood fragments, goose droppings, bits of ash, lead, nitrogen, calcite, plutonium; each era preserved in stripes of mud as far down as the faintest star is up. This is a record that cannot be undone, like guilt you feel but cannot see, that you bury like lake layers so deep it seems unreachable. It is not. Winnow it in your basket, toss it and let the wind blow away the chaff. This is what is worth coming back for, this is what is worth telling you.

Six of Swords

2006

Lily

Old women are rarely pretty; Lily Tuttle was the exception. Her thinness was part of the prettiness. It exposed her cheek bones and accentuated her graceful neck. Maybe that was why she had lived so long, she thought; she never ate much.

Lily was more than ninety, her hair now silver against the black of her younger self, the Gaul in her. A seaside cottage on Canada's eastern coast was her home, wind torn and mottled gray with stunted trees and massive rocks. From her kitchen window she watched the buds leaf out and die, the ground freeze and thaw, waves rise and fall. Little changed year to year. But in the built world there was always something new: computers, multiplexes, assisted living facilities.

As she always had, she kept the little table and its blue cloth by the window. Her tarot cards had soft creases like old skin from decades of use. Lily had always lived with her spirits around her, but now, gauzy, distant hands held her as she slept, moved her fingers as she lit the oven, turned the pages of her book, tuned down the comforter, lifted her body in the bath. The curtain drawn around her world was translucent like the thin edge of a shell. Shadows and shapes darted when she blinked. A sudden warm rush of air, the touch of a wing or finger on her neck. They were close, she was close. How much longer? But each day when she opened her eyes she was still here, still in her cottage, alone. She'd raise herself up and take her swollen feet to the kitchen to boil the coffee and start again. Each breath seemed a conspiracy.

She thought sometimes it was her grief that willed her spirits into being. She'd lost so many by living so long. Her grief was everywhere, in everything, and she'd come to expect it, live within it, and appreciate it. Grief reminded her that she had loved. Grief reminded her that she was not alone, had never been alone.

Lily lit a candle, lay her cards on the table, and let her eyes lose focus. In only moments—she'd done this so many times before—her people were all there: Mother, Uncle Remy, her late-in-life loves, Rafe and Claude. And Harley, her beloved Harley, with her always. But today there was another.

She turned a card face up, caressing its smoothness, its talc-coated comfort. Six of Swords: the navigator, sailing across the water, six tall blades driven into the bottom of the boat.

Mavis. The other woman in Harley's life.

Lily could sense Mavis's presence outside her field of vision. She could hear her, though the voice made no sound. *What violence do we endure?* Mavis asked. *What violence are we capable of?* The candle flickered—cracks in the windowpanes. The answer, an arc shooting across the room: *all of it.*

The image of what Mavis must have looked like came to Lily. Dark-haired, muscular, gray-eyed. Mavis Staunch died a hundred years ago, but Lily knew her like a sister. She closed her eyes to listen.

After the justice's wake I was angry; people had been cruel. It was raining a cold, pricking rain. I stopped for a moment at the overhang of the apothecary to take a breath and calm myself. I saw Angus Epps across the street. I followed him out of town, just as he'd followed me home. I followed him through the woods to the trestle bridge north of the falls. I hid below. I saw him stand between the supports and piss off the side of the bridge. I saw him stumble, I heard him curse, I saw him grasp for the struts, I heard him yell, I saw him fall twenty feet onto the rocks below.

I climbed down the bank to the riverbed where he lay. His leg bones were cracked and bent inhuman. His chest was split open and wet. I smelled him, his shit, his blood. But his eyes were open. He was panting. He was alive.

I straddled him with my thighs. I took the hem of my skirt and stuffed it into his mouth as far as it would go. His eyes widened. Then I pinched his nostrils closed and waited. I pulled his eye open with thumb and forefinger. I wanted him to see me, to see that it was me that was doing this. I waited. It took some time. A minute, two. There were spasms in his body, but I rode him until the eye went milk-gray and every-thing about him stopped. I covered his body with river stones. I was soaked to the bone. I walked home and sat by the wood-stove until I dried through all my layers. Then I paddled out into the lake to think. To find some peace.

An icicle fell to the hard ground and shattered, the sound of thin glass cracking. Lily drew in a sharp breath.

Harley cut my canoe, yes. But I was the one who buttoned my dozens of buttons, doubled-knotted and laced my boots, tied my undergarments tight. It was my own fear that drowned me. My own clothes. Not a ten-year-old boy. Not what I did to Angus.

Lily felt the room shift and knew she was alone again. She snuffed her candle and stared out the window into the day, alive with wind. A new lightness filled her, and for the first time in years she laughed out loud, startling the sparrows in

the hedge, who banked high above the firs, circled, and disappeared into the barren field, digging, she supposed, for
anything that could sustain them. Within moments, another
presence arrived, a warm one.

Did you hear that, Harley? she said. She doesn't blame you.
She never blamed you. Lily felt him there in the room with
her, young and abashed, her nervous lover, his hand cupping
breast, fingers still at last.

*Do you hear the lake singing, Lily? It's the water wash-
ing over us, bathing us like baptism, a blue just born and
becoming.*

I do, Harley. I do. And Lily let her head rest back on her
chair and opened her hands to welcome it.

Acknowledgments

I am incredibly grateful to Deesha Philyaw for selecting *Lake Song* for publication, and I deeply appreciate the time and thought she gave to it. Thank you, thank you. I also need to thank all the folks at Mad Creek who turn manuscript pages into beautiful books. To all of you, and to James Tate Hill and AWP, I am grateful beyond words.

I am indebted to Tom Packard, who first told me about the Burned-Over District and steered me to Whitney R. Cross's book of the same name, which inspired this project. I would not have been able to discover so many details of the Finger Lakes region in the early- and mid-20th century without the wonderful resources of the Penn Yan Historical Society.

To you who read early drafts, I think you know how much I appreciate your insight: thank you Sammy Greenspan, David Desjardins, Jane Sherwin, Elizabeth Brogden, and Lynne Weiss. I owe huge amounts of gratitude to the ever-supportive Elisabeth McKetta; your wise eyes are always a gift. My thanks also to Susan Mills, Michele Mortimer, and my forever friend Meg Ruley for being so generous with your time and thoughts, and to my husband, Gary Duehr. You always make things better.

"Fourth of July" was a finalist in the 2024 *Prime Number Magazine* Award for Short Fiction, "Coaxing Sugar from the Trees" was short listed for the Fish Publishing 23/24 Short Story Prize (Ireland), and "Galen, On the Clyde River" was a 2023 *Sewanee Review* Fiction Contest finalist and was first published as "Mad Lil" in *Pangyrus* in January 2024.

This book is the winner of the 2024 Grace Paley Prize for Short Fiction, part of the Association of Writers & Writing Programs (AWP) Award Series. AWP is a nonprofit organization dedicated to amplifying the voices of writers and the academic programs and organizations that serve them. Please visit www.awpwriter.org for more information.

GRACE PALEY PRIZE FOR SHORT FICTION

Lake Song: A Novel in Stories
LESLEY PRATT BANNATYNE